STORIES ON ANIMALS

Stories on

ANIMALS

PREMCHAND

Edited with an Introduction by
M. Asaduddin

Translated from Hindi and Urdu by
M. Asaduddin and others

PENGUIN
VIKING
An imprint of Penguin Random House

VIKING

USA | Canada | UK | Ireland | Australia
New Zealand | India | South Africa | China

Viking is part of the Penguin Random House group of companies
whose addresses can be found at global.penguinrandomhouse.com

Published by Penguin Random House India Pvt. Ltd
7th Floor, Infinity Tower C, DLF Cyber City,
Gurgaon 122 002, Haryana, India

Published in Viking by Penguin Random House India 2018

These stories were first published as *Premchand: The Complete
Short Stories Volumes 1-4* in Penguin Books 2017

Introduction copyright © M. Asaduddin 2018
The copyright for the English translation vests with the respective translators.

ISBN 9780670091478

Typeset in Adobe Garamond Pro by Manipal Digital Systems, Manipal
Printed at Replika Press Pvt. Ltd, India

www.penguin.co.in

Contents

Introduction

Premchand is generally regarded as the greatest writer in Urdu and Hindi both in terms of his popularity and the range and depth of his corpus. His enduring appeal cuts across class, caste and social groups. He was not only a creative writer in Urdu and Hindi, but fashioned modern prose in both and influenced several generations of writers. The fact that his works were published in more than two dozen Hindi and Urdu journals simultaneously attest to his extraordinary reach to a wide audience that formed his readership. Many of his readers encountered modern Urdu and Hindi novels and short stories, and indeed any literary form, for the first time through his writings. Premchand's unique contribution to the formation of a readership—and, in turn, to shaping the taste of that readership—is yet to be assessed fully. Few or none of his contemporaries in Urdu–Hindi have remained as relevant today as he is in the contexts of the Woman Question (*Stree Vimarsh*), Dalit Discourse (*Dalit Vimarsh*), Gandhian Nationalism, Hindu–Muslim relations and the current debates about the idea of an inclusive India.

Born Dhanpat Rai (1880–1936) in Lamhi, a few miles from Banaras, Premchand's childhood was spent in the countryside. Called 'Nawab' at home, his early schooling was in Urdu and Persian, much in the Kayastha tradition of the time. He also attended the mission school where he studied English along with other subjects. His father was a postal clerk who moved from place to place. When Premchand was only seven his mother died and his father remarried. His relationship with his stepmother was never cordial. He was married at an early age against his wish to a girl who was totally incompatible and he refused to live with her. His second marriage, to a young widow with literary interests, Shivrani, proved to be a happy one. When he was seventeen his father suddenly died and the responsibility of running the family fell on him. He was forced to discontinue his studies and take up the job of a school teacher. However, after his graduation in 1904 he became a sub-deputy inspector of schools, a job which required substantial travel which did not agree with his frail health. In 1921, he gave up government service at the call of Gandhi during the Non-Cooperation movement.

Premchand began writing in 1905 and contributed articles on literary and other subjects in the Urdu journal *Zamana*. His first short stories were also published in this journal. In fact, Premchand began his career as a short story writer with the publication of *Soz-e-Watan* (Lament for the Motherland, 1908), written under his pen name, Nawab Rai. The collection drew the attention of the colonial government because of its alleged radical intent. He was summoned, when he was on an inspection tour, to explain his position. This is how Premchand describes the situation in his own words:

> . . . Those days I wrote under the name of Nawab Rai. I already had some information that the intelligence wing of the police was making inquiries to track down the author of the book. I could realize that they have found me out and I had been summoned to defend myself.
>
> The Saheb asked, 'Have you written this book?' I admitted that I had.
>
> The Saheb then asked me to explain the subject matter of each story, and finally burst out in anger, 'Your stories are full of sedition. Thank God that you are a servant of the British Empire. Had this happened during the Mughal rule both your hands would have been chopped off.'[1]

He was asked to burn all the copies of the book, and henceforth, get prior permission from the administration before sending any writing for publication. Petrified, he abided by the demands of the magistrate and submitted all available copies of the book to his office to be destroyed. Premchand realized that writing under the name Nawab Rai was no longer safe and sustainable, and to circumvent the iron hand of colonial censorship he had to assume a new pseudonym, which was Premchand. Thus, both Dhanpat Rai and Nawab Rai were

---

[1] 'Munshi Premchand ki Kahani Unki Zubani' in *Zamana* (Premchand Number), 1938. Reprinted by National Council for Promotion of Urdu Language, July 2002, p.54.

finally buried and Premchand was born, a name by which
generations of readers would know him.

Themes

Caste

Premchand felt a deep affinity with the common man and
his natural sympathy was towards the oppressed and deprived
sections of society. No writer before him in Urdu or Hindi,
and possibly other Indian literatures, had depicted the lives of
the underdogs, the untouchables and the marginalized with
such depth and empathy. Throughout his life 'Premchand
did not let go of his unsentimental awareness of the grim
realities of rural life, of life at the bottom of the economic scale'
(Amrit Rai: 1982, ix). The oppressors and oppression came
in many forms—they may have been priests or zamindars,
lawyers or policemen or even doctors, all of whom held the
society in their strangle-hold. Rituals pertaining to Hindu
marriages and death were so exploitative and oppressive that
these events were often robbed of their dignity and joy and
spelt the ruin of families.

Premchand began his career by exposing the corruption
of the Hindu priestly class in his novel *Asraar-e-Muavid*
(Mysteries of the House of Worship, 1903–05), and then
he continued the tirade in many of his stories. In the story
'Babaji's Feast' 'Babaji ka Bhog' he depicts the greed of the
Brahmin baba who has no compunction in robbing a poor
family of its meagre means, and in 'Funeral Feast' 'Mritak
Bhoj' he showed how the predatory and parasitical Brahmins
drive another Brahmin woman to destitution and her

daughter to suicide. In a series of stories where the central character is Moteram, a Brahmin priest, Premchand exposes with rare courage the rapacity, the hollowness and hypocrisy of the Hindu priestly class, which earned him the ire and venom of a section of high-caste Hindus, even culminating in a law suit for defamation. But he remained undaunted and went on exposing many oppressive customs that were prevalent in society.

But his most trenchant critique was reserved for caste injustice whereby people at the lowest rung of the Hindu caste system were considered untouchables and were compelled to live a life of indignity and humiliation. The upper-caste Hindus treated them as worse than animals and this injustice was institutionalized through social sanction of the caste system. Stories such as 'The Well of the Thakur' 'Thakur ka Kuan', 'Salvation' 'Sadgati', 'Shroud' 'Kafan', 'Temple' 'Mandir', 'The Woman Who Sold Grass' 'Ghaaswali' and 'One and a Quarter Ser of Wheat' 'Sawa Ser Gehun' constitute a devastating indictment of the way the upper-caste Hindus have treated the Dalits for generations. The stories demonstrate that the Dalits were subjected to daily humiliation by members of the upper castes and this humiliation stemmed from the fact that Dalit inferiority had become embedded in the psyche of the members of the Hindu upper castes who had developed a vast repertoire of idioms, symbols and gestures of verbal and physical denigration of the Dalits over centuries. Grave injustice and inhuman treatment of the Dalits had become normalized, causing no revulsion against it in society. Despite criticism from some Dalit ideologues levelling some rather irresponsible charges against Premchand for depicting Dalits in a certain way, these stories—some of which have been rendered into films—have contributed significantly in raising awareness about the injustice perpetrated against the most vulnerable section of society.

Women

A considerable number of his stories deal with the plight of women. Premchand was deeply sensitive to the suffering of women in a patriarchal society where women had no agency and had to live their lives according to the whims and fancies of men on whom they had to depend—husbands, fathers, brothers or even close or distant male relatives. Women were expected to be docile, submissive and self-effacing, sacrificing their lives for the well-being of the family. Girls were treated as a curse to the family and their parents were subjected to all kinds of humiliations and indignities while arranging their marriage. Parents were sometimes compelled to marry off their nubile and very young daughters to old men just to unburden themselves of the responsibility and shame of being saddled with an unmarried daughter. The practices of *kanya vikray* (sale of a daughter in marriage), even *kanya vadh* (killing of a girl child) too were prevalent.

In his essays and editorials, Premchand made a strong plea for the abolition of the evil practices that made the life of women unbearable. He supported divorce in extreme circumstances, backed the wife's claim to half of the husband's property in case of divorce and inherit the property in case of the husband's death. He also wrote in favour of the Sarda Bill which aimed at raising the minimum age of marriage of girls. In a large number of stories, such as 'Tuliya' 'Devi',

'Sati', 'Goddess from Heaven' 'Swarg ki Devi', 'Return' 'Shanti', 'Godavari's Suicide' 'Saut', 'Thread of Love' 'Prem Sutra', 'Two Friends' 'Do Sakhiyaan', 'The Lunatic' 'Unmaad' and so on, he sheds light on the plight of women in an oppressive, patriarchal system. Through the immortal characters of old women like the Chachi in 'Holy Judges', the Old Aunt in the eponymous story and Bhungi in 'A Positive Change' 'Vidhwans', he shows how difficult life was for old women in a society that was known to respect its elderly members. The fate of widows, who were considered inauspicious and were expected to renounce all joys of life, was even worse, as shown in 'Compulsion' 'Nairashya Leela', 'The Condemned' 'Dhikkar' and 'A Widow with Sons' 'Betonwali Vidhva'.

The Village and the City

Premchand's love for the countryside is evident in his fictional and non-fictional writings. He has written several extremely evocative stories such as 'Panchayat', 'Do Bail', 'Idgah', 'Atma Ram', depicting the pristine village life of simplicity, honesty and quiet contentment. In fact, his fictional corpus, if read uncritically, would lend itself to an easy binary between country life and city life, one good and the other almost irredeemably evil. Yet, we have to recognize that he does not depict country life as an idyll shorn of all evils. There are stories such as 'A Positive Change' 'Vidhwans', 'A Home for an Orphan' 'Grihdaah' and 'The Road to Salvation' 'Mukti Marg' that de-romanticize and demystify village life and depict the author's awareness of the imperfections and blind spots in the supposed idyll. Thus, the apparent binary that seems to work in case of some novels and stories cannot be stretched beyond a point.

Animals

Premchand's deep interest in the simple life of peasants extended to his love for animals, particularly draught animals, treated most cruelly in India. Very few writers have depicted such an intimate bond between animals and human beings. Premchand depicts animals as endowed with emotions just as human beings are, responding to love and affection just as human beings do, and are fully deserving of human compassion. Often, the duplicity, cruelty and betrayal in the human world is contrasted with the unconditional love and loyalty displayed by animals towards their masters and those who care for them. It is a heart-wrenching moment, as shown in 'Money for Deliverance' 'Muktidhan' and 'Sacrifice' 'Qurbani' when a peasant has to part with his animals because of want and destitution. The deep compassion with which animal life has been depicted in 'Holy Judges' 'Panchayat' 'Reincarnation' 'Purva Sanskar' 'The Story of Two Bullocks' 'Do Bailon ki Katha' and 'The Roaming Monkey' 'Salilani Bandar' are treasures of world literature. Stories such as 'Turf War' 'Adhikar Chinta' and 'Defending One's Liberty' 'Swatt Raksha', written in a humorous and symbolic vein, show how a dog fiercely protects his turf and how a horse defeats all the machinations of human beings to make him work on a Sunday which is his day of rest, rightfully earned after working for six days of the week! In 'The Roaming Monkey', the author shows how a monkey earns money by showing tricks of different kinds and thus looks after the wife of his owner, nurtures her and brings her back from the brink of lunacy. In 'The Price of Milk' 'Doodh ki Qeemat' we have the spectacle of goats feeding a baby with milk from their own udders, thereby saving its life.

Premchand's Style

The atmosphere of dastaan and historical romances hangs heavy on Premchand's early stories. But he soon grew out of that phase and made his work more socially relevant by giving it the hard, gritty texture of realism. His art of storytelling became a vehicle for his socially engaged agenda of social reform and ameliorating the condition of the deprived and oppressed sections of society. However, that does not mean he was mainly concerned with the content and external circumstances of his characters and not with their inner worlds. Like all great writers, he took interest in unravelling the mental processes of his characters and the psychological motivations of their actions. As he says:

> My stories are usually based on some observations or personal experience. I try to introduce some dramatic elements in them. I do not write stories merely to describe an event. I try to express some philosophical/emotional reality through them. As long as I do not find any such basis I cannot put my pen to paper. When this is settled, I conceive characters. Sometimes, studying history brings some plots to mind. An event does not form a story, as long as it does not express a psychological view of reality.[2]

---

[2] 'Premchand ki Afsana Nigari', *Zamana*: Premchand Issue, February 1938; rpt. National Council for Promotion of Urdu (New Delhi, 2002), p. 173.

In the stories he has written one finds different modes and points of view, which he adopted by employing an array of narrative devices. An overwhelming number of his stories are written in the third person or omniscient narrative mode and a far lesser number in the first person. He makes extensive use of dialogue, using different registers of Urdu and Hindi in addition to dialects, colloquialisms, idioms and speech patterns specific to a caste, class or community. He also uses the technique of interior monologue and multiple points of view in quite a few stories. The salient point is that even though Premchand was mainly concerned with the content of his stories, to the extent of sometimes making them formulaic and predictable, he certainly did engage with the stylistic aspects too. And in this respect, he was influenced by both Indian—specifically Bengali—and foreign writers.

M. Asaduddin

The Story of Two Bullocks

1

The jackass is taken to be the most stupid of animals. Whenever we want to say that someone is a fool of the first order we call him a jackass. One cannot really say whether the jackass is stupid, or his harmless nature has earned him this title.

Cows strike with their horns, and a newly calved one can easily assume the aspect of a lioness. The dog is also a helpless creature, but he too feels angry at times. One has, however, never heard or seen a jackass getting into a rage. Thrash him as much as you want, give him the worst kind of grass that has gone stale—but you will never see the merest shadow of discontent on his face. He might prance around a bit in the month of Baisakh, but I have never seen a jackass to be truly happy. Melancholy sits on his face permanently. He does not change in moments of joy or sorrow, profit or loss. The attributes of god-men and sages seem to have reached their climax in the jackass, yet people call him a fool. Such disrespect for virtue cannot be seen anywhere else.

Sometimes, simplicity does not help in this world. Look now, why are Indians in Africa in such a pitiable state? Why aren't they allowed to enter America? The poor fellows do not drink liquor, they save up some money for bad times, they work really hard and never get into brawls with anyone. Even when insulted they do not retaliate, but still they are given a bad name. It is said that they lower the standard of living. If they had learnt to fight back they would probably have been called civilized. The example of Japan is there—a single victory and they are now treated among the civilized nations of the world.

But the jackass has a younger brother who is just a little lower in the scale of stupidity, and he is the bullock. We use the phrase 'calf's uncle' in more or less the same sense that we use jackass. Some people might call the bullock the greatest among fools, but our views are different. Sometimes the bullock strikes back, and one also witnesses the spectacle of a raging bullock. In several other ways he does express his discontent; hence he must be ranked lower than the jackass.

Jhuri, the vegetable farmer, had named his two bullocks Hira and Moti. They were of western stock—good-looking, of good stature and agile in work. Having lived together a long time, they had become like brothers. Facing each other or sitting side by side they would exchange views in their silent language. How one understood the other's feelings we cannot say. They must have been endowed with a secret power, unknown to human beings who claim to be the noblest of all beings. They expressed their love by licking and sniffing each other. Sometimes they would lock their horns, not in enmity but in affection and familiarity, the way intimate friends hug or slap each other's backs tightly. Without it the friendship lacks verve, as if it was hollow and cannot be trusted. When these two were yoked together in the plough or the cart and they walked along swinging their necks, each strove to carry the greater part of the burden on his shoulder. After the day's work they would unwind in the afternoon or the evening, and tried to alleviate their fatigue by licking one another. When the oilcakes and the straw were thrown into the manger they would stand up together, thrust their muzzles into the manger and then sit down side by side. When one withdrew his mouth from the trough, the other did the same.

It happened on one occasion that Jhuri sent the bullocks to his father-in-law's. Now, how would the bullocks know why they were sent away? They thought that they had been sold off by their master. No one knew whether they liked being sold off in this way, but Jhuri's brother-in-law, Gaya, had a tough time leading them away. If he hollered from behind they would run right or left, and if he pulled them holding the rope from the front they would pull back. If he thrashed them they would lower their heads and bellow. If God had given them speech they would have asked Jhuri, 'Why are you driving us, poor wretches, away? We have tried our best to serve you. If you were not satisfied with the amount of work, we could've done more. We would have preferred to die in your service. We never complained about the fodder. We ate whatever you gave us. Then why did you sell us off to this tyrant?'

The two reached their new home in the evening. They had been starving the whole day but when they were brought to the trough, neither of them so much as sniffed the fodder. Their hearts were heavy; they had been separated from the place they regarded as home. The new house, new village, new people—all seemed alien to them.

They consulted each other in their mute language, glanced at one another from the corners of their eyes and then lay down. When the entire village was in deep slumber, they pulled hard, broke the tether and set out for home. The tether was a tough one, no one could have thought that any bullock could break it. But the two bullocks found their energy redoubled at the moment and the tether gave way to their violent jerks.

When Jhuri got up in the morning he saw the two bullocks standing at the trough, a part of the tether dangling from their necks. Their legs were covered with slush up to the knees and their eyes shone with rebellious affection.

His heart welled up with affection at this sight. He ran to the trough and threw his arms around them. The spectacle of him kissing and hugging them by turns was a heart-warming sight.

The children of his house and the village gathered there and welcomed the bullocks by clapping their hands. This incident, though not without precedent in the village, had its significance. The assembly of boys decided that these two animal-heroes deserved formal congratulations. They brought bread, molasses, bran and chaff from their houses.

One of them said, 'No one has bullocks like these.'

Another boy replied, 'Yes indeed. They managed to come back from so far on their own.'

A third one butted in, 'They aren't bullocks. They must have been human beings in their earlier birth.'

No one dared to dispute this.

When Jhuri's wife saw the bullocks at the door she flared up. 'How ungrateful these bullocks are! They didn't work even for a day before running away.'

Jhuri could not listen to this accusation hurled at his bullocks. 'Why are you calling them ungrateful? Your people must not have given them food, so what they could do?'

His wife said aggressively, 'Yes, it is only you who know how to feed the bullocks. Other people simply feed their animals water.'

Jhuri mocked her, 'Why would they run off if they were given fodder?'

His wife was peeved. 'They ran off because my people do not fondle them like fools as you do. If they feed them, they also make them work hard. These two are shirkers, so they ran away. Now, I'll see who gives them oilcakes and bran. I'll give them nothing but dry straw. They can eat it or die!'

This is exactly what came about. The servants were told that the bullocks should be given only dry straw.

When the bullocks thrust their mouths in the trough their food seemed insipid. No flavour, no juice. How could they eat? They began to gaze at the door with longing eyes.

Jhuri said to a servant, 'Hey, why aren't you throwing some oilseeds?'

'The mistress will kill me.'

'You can do it on the sly.'

'No, Dada. Later you'll also side with her.'

2

The brother-in-law of Jhuri arrived the next day and took away the bullocks. This time he yoked them both to his cart.

Twice or thrice Moti tried to pull the cart to the ditch along the road but Hira held him back. Hira was more patient.

Reaching home in the evening Gaya tied them with thick ropes as a punishment for the previous day's mischief. Then he threw the same dry straw at them. To his own two bullocks he gave oilseed cakes and other delicacies.

The bullocks had never faced such humiliation. Jhuri wouldn't strike them even with a flower stick. He would merely click his tongue and they would run. Here they were thrashed. Their honour was bruised; on top of it they were given only dry straw to eat.

They didn't even look at the trough.

The next day Gaya yoked them to the plough. But it was as if they had sworn not to budge from where they stood. Once when the cruel fellow struck Hira on his nostrils, Moti went mad with rage and ran away with the plough. The ploughshare, the yoke, the rope, the harness were all smashed to pieces. But for the thick ropes around their necks no one could have caught them.

Hira said in his mute language, 'It is useless to run away.'

Moti replied, 'But he almost killed you.'

'Now he'll beat us to his heart's content.'

'Let him. We were born bullocks, how long can we escape beating?'

'Gaya is running towards us with two other fellows. They've sticks in their hands.'

Moti said, 'Shall I show him a few tricks. He's coming with a stick.'

Hira reasoned with him, 'No, brother. Stand still.'

'If he beats me, I'll knock one or two down.'

'No. This isn't our dharma.'

Moti stood there resentfully. Gaya arrived and led them away. Fortunately, he didn't beat them, for if he had, Moti would have struck back. Seeing his frown Gaya and his companions decided that it was better to put it off this time.

The same dry straw was thrown at them again, but they stood immobile. The people in the house started their meal. At that moment, a small girl came out holding two rotis in her hand. She fed them the rotis and went away. One roti was scarcely sufficient to appease their hunger but they felt a sense of contentment in their hearts. Here, too, lived someone who was decent and humane. The girl was Bhairo's daughter who had lost her mother. Her stepmother used to beat her often, so that is why she felt a kind of kinship with the bullocks.

Both remained yoked to the harness throughout the day, were thrashed and sometimes they acted stubbornly. In the evening, they were tied up at their stall, and at night the same small girl fed them two rotis. For them, it was like blessed food, consecrated by love, which gave them strength so that they didn't grow weak on the daily dole of a few mouthfuls of straw. But their eyes and every pore of their body exuded rebellion.

One day, Moti said in his mute language, 'I can't put up with it any more, Hira.'

'What do you want to do?'

'Want to lift one or two on my horns and toss them.'

'You know very well that the owner of this house is the father of the dear girl who feeds us rotis. Won't the poor girl become an orphan?'

'Should I toss the mistress, then? It is she who beats the girl.'

'You're forgetting that it is forbidden to strike womankind.'

'You leave no way out for me. Tell me, shall we break the rope and run off?'

'Yes, I'd agree to that. But how can you break such a strong rope?'

'There's a way. First chew the rope a little, then give a tug.'

At night when the girl left after feeding them rotis, both started gnawing at the rope. But the big rope slipped away from their mouths. They tried again and again without any luck.

Suddenly the door opened and the girl came out. Both lowered their heads and began to lick the girl's palm. Their tails stood up as she stroked their foreheads. Then she said, 'I'm untying the rope. You must run away quietly, or these people will kill you. Today, they were talking about putting rings in your noses.'

She untied the knot, but they stood there transfixed.

Moti said in his own language, 'Why don't you move now?'

Hira said, 'We can run away, but tomorrow this girl will be in trouble. Everyone will suspect her.'

Suddenly the girl yelled out, 'Uncle's bullocks are running away! Daddy, daddy, hurry up! They're running off!'

Gaya rushed out of the house and ran to catch the bullocks. They broke into a sprint with Gaya in hot pursuit. They ran faster and Gaya raised an alarm. Then he turned back to fetch some fellows from the village. The two friends took the opportunity to make good their escape. They ran straight ahead, oblivious of the right way. They could not find any trace of the familiar way they had come through. They encountered new villages. Then they stood at the edge of a field and began to think about what they should do next.

Hira said, 'It seems we've lost our way.'

'You ran without thinking. We should have knocked him dead right there.'

'If we had done that what would the world say? He abandoned his dharma, why should we abandon ours?'

They were going numb with hunger. The field had peas growing in it and they began to help themselves, at times stopping to listen if anyone was coming.

When they had had their fill they were overwhelmed by their new-found independence and began to caper and jump about. First, they belched, then they locked their horns and began to push one another around. Moti pushed Hira back several steps until he fell into a ditch. That made even Hira angry. He somehow managed to get up and clashed with Moti. Moti saw that what began as a game was turning into a brawl and drew aside.

3

Now, what did they see? A raging bull was heading towards them. Yes, indeed, it was a bull and it had almost reached where they stood. The two friends were in a tight spot and looked for an escape route. The bull looked like a veritable elephant. To clash with him would be fatal. But even if they did not clash with him, there did not seem to be any chance of their survival. He was heading straight towards them. It was a monstrous sight!

Moti said in his mute language, 'We are in a tight spot. Can we save our skin? Think of some way.'

Hira said in a worried voice, 'He is blind with pride and won't listen to our pleas.'

'Let's run.'

'Running away is cowardice.'

'Then you die here. I'm taking to my heels.'

'And if he chases us?'

'Then think of something else.'

'The only way out is—we pounce on him together at once. I'll lead the attack from the front, you take him from behind. Cornered from both sides, he'll take to his heels. If he jumps on me, you thrust your horns in his belly from the side. Our lives are on the line, but there's no other way.'

Taking courage in both hands the two friends mounted the attack. The bull had no experience of facing a united army. He was accustomed to fighting duels. The moment he leapt at Hira, Moti gave him chase from behind. The bull turned back to face him when Hira pounced on him. The bull wanted to knock them down one by one, but these two were masters of their craft and did not give him the opportunity. Infuriated by this two-pronged attack, the bull at one point moved menacingly towards Hira, determined to make short work of him, but right at that moment Moti came from sideways and thrust his horns into his belly. The bull turned back furiously when Hira attacked him with his horns from the other side. Badly injured, the bull took to his heels and the two friends chased him for quite some distance until the bull collapsed on the ground, unconscious. Then they left him.

Intoxicated by the victory the two friends walked triumphantly, swinging from side to side.

Moti said in his symbolic language, 'I really wanted to finish off the fellow.'

Hari reprimanded him, 'One should not strike a fallen enemy.'

'This is rubbish. The enemy should be struck down in a way that he does not rise again.'

'Now, how to get back home—think about that.'

'Let's first eat something and think later.'

The pea field was spread right before them. Moti went crashing in. Hira forbade him but he didn't listen. He had barely taken two or three morsels when two men appeared with sticks and surrounded the two friends. Hira was standing on the embankment and ran away, but Moti was deep in the soggy field. His hooves got stuck in the mud so he could not escape and was caught. When Hira saw that his friend was in trouble, he came back. If they were going to be trapped, they would be trapped together. The watchmen caught him too.

In the morning the two friends were shut up in the pound.

4

The whole day passed by and they were not given even a single straw to eat—this was the first time in their lives that such a thing had happened. They did not understand what kind of master it was. There were several buffaloes, goats, horses and donkeys, but no one had any fodder before them. All were lying on the ground like corpses. Some of them were so weak that they could not even stand. The two friends kept their gaze fixed at the gate the entire day but no one appeared with food. Then both began to lick the sultry clay of the wall but that could hardly bring them any satisfaction.

When they were not given any food in the evening too, the flame of rebellion flared up in Hira's heart. He said to Moti, 'I can't bear it any more.'

His head lowered, Moti answered, 'I feel as though my life is ebbing out.'

'Don't give up so quickly, buddy. We must find some way of getting out of here.'

'Come, let's break the wall.'

'I'm not good for anything now.'

'Well, why did you then brag about your strength?'

'All bragging has gone out of me now.'

The wall of the enclosure was built of clay. Hira was strong, he thrust his pointed horn against the wall. When he dug deeper a big chunk of clay came loose. This encouraged him. Running again and again he hit the wall and with every blow he knocked off little chunks of clay from the wall.

Right at that hour the pound watchman came holding the lantern in his hand to take his daily count of the animals. When he saw Hira in his rebellious mood he dealt him several blows and then tied him up with a thick rope.

Moti said from where he lay, 'What did you get out of it except a beating?'

'Well, at least I tried to use my strength.'

'What use was it when you got tied up as a consequence?'

'Well, we must use our power whatever the consequence.'

'In that case, you may end up paying with your life.'

'I don't care. We're going to die anyway. Just think if the wall had come down how many lives could have been saved. So many of our brothers are locked up here. There is hardly any life left in their bodies. If it continues like this for a couple of days more, they'll all die.'

'That's true. All right then, let me also use my strength.'

Moti also struck the wall at the same spot. A lump of clay fell down which gave him encouragement. He began to strike the wall repeatedly as though it was his sworn adversary. Finally, after about two hours of struggle the top of the wall came down by about a foot and a half. He dealt a final blow with redoubled strength and this time half of the wall came crashing down.

As soon as the wall came down, the animals who had been lying like corpses for so long got up. The three mares galloped away first, followed by the goats. Then the buffaloes slipped away, but the donkeys were still lying there as before.

Hira asked, 'Why aren't you two running away?'

One of them replied, 'What if we get caught again?'

'What does it matter? At least now you've got the opportunity to escape.'

'We're scared. We'd rather stay where we are.'

It was well past midnight. The two donkeys were still thinking whether they should escape or not. Moti was busy trying to chew his friend's rope. When he gave up, Hira said, 'You go. Let me stay here. Maybe, we'll meet again sometime.'

With his eyes brimming over, Moti said, 'Do you think I'm so selfish, Hira? You and I have been together for such a long time! If you're in trouble today can I just run away and leave you alone?'

Hira said, 'They'll thrash you really hard. They will understand that it's your handiwork.'

Moti said proudly, 'If I get thrashed for the crime for which they have tied you, I don't give a damn. At least this much has been achieved that the lives of nine or ten animals have been saved. They'll bless us.'

Saying this Moti shoved the two donkeys with his horns and drove them out of the enclosure. Then he lay beside his friend and went to sleep.

There is no need to describe the chaotic scene that ensued in the morning when the clerk, the watchman and the other officials saw what had happened. Suffice it to say that Moti was roundly thrashed and he too was tied up with a large rope.

5

For a whole week the two friends stayed tied up there. No one gave them even a bit of straw. They were just given water once which helped them survive. They grew so weak that they could hardly stand, and their ribs stuck out of their skins.

One day, they heard the sound of drums in front of the enclosure, and by noon about fifty to sixty people gathered there. Then the two friends were taken out and the inspection began. People came to have a look at them and went back disappointed. Who would be interested in buying bullocks that looked like corpses?

Suddenly a bearded man appeared there whose eyes were red and who had a ruthless look. He poked his fingers at the haunches of the bullocks and began to talk with the clerk. The appearance of the man made the two friends shudder. They had no doubt who he was and why he was groping their bodies. They looked at each other with frightened eyes and lowered their heads.

Hira said, 'It was futile to run away from Gaya's house. We can't save our heads now.'

Moti said irreverently, 'It is said that God is kind to everybody. Why isn't He kind to us?'

'For God, it does not matter whether we live or die. In a way, it's good that for a while we'll be with Him. Once God had saved us in the form of that little girl. Won't He save us now?'

'This man is going to slash us with his knife. Just watch out.'

'Well, why worry? Our flesh, hide, horns and bones will be of use to someone or the other.'

After the auction both friends went off with the bearded fellow. Every pore of their bodies trembled in fear. They had no strength to lift their hooves but they were so frightened that they staggered along—for if they slowed down a little, the fellow would serve them a sharp lash.

Along the way they saw a verdant meadow where cows and bullocks were grazing. All the animals were happy, good-looking and full of zest. Some were leaping while others were joyfully chewing the cud sitting leisurely. How happy they were! And how selfish! In their blissful state, they did not care that two of their brothers . . .

Suddenly it seemed to them that the road was familiar. Yes, it was the same road by which Gaya had led them away. They saw the same fields, orchards and villages. With every step their pace quickened. Their fatigue and weakness disappeared. Oh, look, here was their own pasture, and here was the well from which they pulled water by working the winch. It was the same well.

Moti said, 'Our house is close by.'

'It's all God's kindness,' responded Hira.

'I'm making a run for home.'

'Will he allow you?'

'I'll knock him down.'

'Oh no! Let's run and reach our stalls, and we won't budge from there.'

They seemed to go crazy with delight, and like calves, leaped and ran towards the house. 'That's our stall!' They reached the spot and stood there. The bearded fellow also followed them.

Jhuri was sitting in his doorway sunning himself. As soon as he saw the bullocks he ran to them and began hugging them over and over again. Tears of joy streamed down the eyes of the two friends, and one of them started licking Jhuri's hand.

The bearded fellow came up and grabbed the tethers tied to the bullocks' necks.

Jhuri said, 'They are my bullocks.'

'How can they be? I bought them over in the auction at the animal pound.'

'I think you have stolen them,' said Jhuri. 'Just leave quietly. They are my bullocks. Only I have the right to sell them. No one else has the right to sell my bullocks in an auction.'

'I'll complain at the police station.'

'They're mine. The surest proof is that they're standing at my door.'

Infuriated, the bearded fellow advanced and tried to drag the bullocks by force. Right at that moment Moti struck with his horns. The fellow stepped back. Moti chased him. He stopped only when had driven the fellow out of the village, and then stood there guarding the way. The man stood at some distance threatening, cursing and pelting stones at Moti. And Moti stood there like a victorious hero, blocking the way. The villagers had gathered there to see the spectacle and had a hearty laugh.

When the butcher admitted defeat and went away Moti walked back swaggering.

Hira said, 'I was afraid you might bump him off in anger.'

'If he had grabbed me, I would've certainly killed him.'

'He won't come back now.'

'If he does, I'll take care of him. I'll see how he takes us away.'

'What if he gets us shot?'

'Well, I'll die but I'll be of no use to him.'

'Nobody thinks our life is worth anything.'

'Just because we're so simple.'

Soon the trough was filled with oilseed cakes, straw, bran and grain, and the two friends began to eat. Jhuri started stroking them affectionately while a troupe of boys witnessed the spectacle.

Just then the mistress of the house emerged and kissed the two on their foreheads.

Translated from the Hindi by M. Asaduddin

Money for Deliverance

1

Of all the trades that we have in India, the business of lending money is the most advantageous. Usually the annual rate of interest is charged at twenty-five per cent but for vast pieces of land or large amounts of money the annual rate of interest is charged at twelve per cent. It is generally impossible to get a loan at a lesser rate of interest. There is hardly any business that provides a profit margin of over fifteen per cent, and that too without much hassle. And apart from the money received from interest, additional expenses like token money, paperwork, brokerage and money spent on court proceedings are also borne by the borrower. All this income, in some way or the other, finds its way into the moneylender's pocket. This is the reason that the business of lending money is on the rise. Advocates, doctors, government employees, landowners; whoever has surplus wealth, can start this business. This is an excellent way to utilize one's savings wisely.

Lala Daudayal was also a moneylender of this category. He worked as a solicitor and lent whatever he saved at twenty-five to thirty per cent of interest a year. He mostly did business with lower-class people. He was cautious of high-class people; he never let them loiter around him. His belief was (and every businessman would support this) that it's better to throw money into a ditch than lend it to a Brahmin, Kshatriya or Kayastha. At the time of receiving the loan they would appear to possess enough wealth to secure the loan, but the moment the money reached their hands, all their wealth seemed to disappear. Their wives, sons or brothers would materialize from somewhere to assert their right on the wealth and it would, in a way, seem that their wealth never actually existed in reality. And their legal preparation was such that many erudite scholars of law would also concede defeat.

One day Daudayal was returning home from court when he witnessed a strange incident. A Muslim man was selling his cow on the road, and many people had surrounded him. Some thrust money in his hands while a few tried to snatch the tether from him, but the poor Muslim man only kept on looking at the faces of the customers and after pondering over something held the tether even more tightly. The cow was a beauty. She had a slender neck, heavy haunches and milk-filled udders. A beautiful, sturdy calf stood by, glued to its mother. The Muslim man seemed extremely agitated and sad. He was looking at the cow with compassion-filled eyes, trying to contain his emotions. Daudayal was delighted to see the cow. He asked, 'Hey, do you want to sell the cow? What's your name?'

When the Muslim man saw Daudayal, he went to him happily and said, 'Yes, sir, I want to sell her.'

'Where have you brought her from? What's your name?'

'My name is Rehman and I live in Pacholi.'

'Does she give milk?'

'Yes, sir, she will give around one kilolitre of milk at a time. She is so good that she allows even a child to milk her. Children keep playing around her feet but that never annoys her.'

'Does anybody know you here?' The solicitor was suspicious, thinking that the cow might be stolen.

'No, sir, I am a poor man, nobody knows me.'

'What is your asking price?'

Rehman asked for fifty rupees. The solicitor felt that thirty rupees was the correct price to strike a deal. For a while both sides haggled. One craved the money while the other craved the cow. It didn't take long to seal the deal. It was fixed at thirty-five rupees.

Rehman had made the deal but he was still ensnared by love. He kept standing there for some time lost in thought, then he began to follow Daudayal with the cow slowly.

Then another man said, 'Hey, I will give you thirty-six rupees. Come with us.'

'I won't give you the cow; you can't force me.'

Another man said, 'Take forty rupees from me . . . that should make you happy, yes?' He tried to take the cow from Rehman's hand, but Rehman did not relent. Finally, everybody left in disappointment.

After a little while Rehman said to Daudayal, 'Sir, you are a Hindu, you will rear her well and take care of her. All those people are merciless; I wouldn't have sold her to them for even fifty rupees. You came on time; otherwise they would have snatched the cow away by force. I have fallen into deep trouble, sir, that is why I had to sell the cow. Otherwise I wouldn't have ever sold her. I have raised her on my own. How could I have sold her to those butchers? Sir, if you feed her oilcakes she will give you ample milk. Even a buffalo's milk is not as sweet and thick as hers. Sir, I have one more request, tell your herdsman not to ever beat her.'

Daudayal looked at Rehman in astonishment. *God! A person of his class has so much goodness and compassion! Even fervent devotees of Lord Shiva and great mahatmas sell cows to brutes to not incur losses of any kind. And this poor man sold the cow to me despite suffering a loss only to ensure she's not mistreated. The poor also possess such wisdom!*

He returned home and gave the money to Rehman. Rehman tied the money in a knot, looked at the cow lovingly once more and took his leave.

Rehman was a poor peasant, and everybody is out to exploit the poor. The landowner had filed a case against him in the court claiming an increased rate of land revenue. Money was required to contest the case in the court. Rehman didn't have any property except for a pair of oxen. He loved the cow more than his life, but as he couldn't arrange for the money, he was forced to sell her.

2

There were many Muslims living in Pacholi. The route to hajj had opened after many years. During the World War in the West the route had been closed. Men and women started to go on hajj again in hordes from the village. Rehman's old mother was also preparing to go on hajj. She said to Rehman, 'Son, I only have one desire left in my heart. I don't want to leave this world without seeing this desire fulfilled. Allah will reward you for it.' Devotion to their mothers is a special characteristic of rural people. Earlier, Rehman had failed to collect enough money to send his mother on hajj but now he dared not ignore her command. He thought of borrowing money from somebody. He reasoned with himself, *Some I will return after harvesting this season's sugar cane crop, the rest I will repay next year. By Allah's grace the sugar cane has grown like never before. This is all because of mother's prayers. But whom should I ask? I need a minimum of two hundred rupees. I do not even know any moneylenders. The few that we have here are always after their customers' lives. Maybe I should go to Lala Daudayal. He is better than the rest. But I have heard that he is known to extract his money back as per the deal, he doesn't relent one bit. If he doesn't get his money back there is no respite for the customer. He starts a dialogue only after he has filed a lawsuit against the customer. Although, it is true that he doesn't cheat his customers . . . he keeps the transaction transparent.*

For many days he was in a fix—should he approach Daudayal or not? What if he was unable to return the money? Daudayal wouldn't relent without dragging him to court. His house, cattle, everything would get auctioned. But having reached his wits' end, he finally went to Daudayal and asked for the loan.

'Weren't you the one who sold the cow to me?'

'Yes, sir.'

'I will lend you the money but you must return it as per your promise. If you fail to keep the deadline then the onus falls on you. I won't give you any concession then. Tell me, when will you return the money?'

Rehman did some calculations in his head and answered, 'Sir, give me two years.'

'If you don't return the money in two years the rate of interest will become thirty-two per cent. I will be generous enough not to file a case against you.'

'Do as you please. I won't run away.'

Rehman got one hundred and eighty rupees instead of two hundred. Some money was deducted for the paperwork, some was kept as token money, and some for brokerage. He returned home and sold some jaggery that was kept in the house. He advised his wife on how to manage the family affairs and left for Mecca with his mother.

3

When the deadline for returning the money passed, Daudayal summoned Rehman to him and said harshly, 'Haven't your two years elapsed? Come on, where is the money?'

Rehman answered piteously, 'Sir, I've fallen on hard times. My mother has been sick ever since she returned from hajj. The entire day I keep running from pillar to post to get her medicines. I just want to be by her side as long as she is alive; work I can do all my life. There was no harvest this time, sir. The sugar cane dried up because it didn't get any water. The other plants in the farm have also wilted. I didn't get enough time to even carry them to the granary. I couldn't even prepare the soil for the spring crop; the seeds are still lying wasted. Allah knows how difficult my days have become. Sir, I will repay each and every penny of yours. Grant me a period of one year. The moment my mother gets better, I'll be back to work.'

'The rate of interest will become thirty-two per cent.'

'As you wish, sir.'

Rehman returned home to find that his mother was on her deathbed. It had become painful for her to even breathe. She only wanted a glimpse of her son, which was fulfilled as soon as he entered. His mother looked at him with fondness, bestowed her blessing on him and departed for heaven. Until then, Rehman had been up to his neck in debt. Now the debt pretty much drowned him.

He borrowed some money from his neighbours for the funeral but in order to provide peace and satisfaction to the soul it was essential to give a portion of one's land as alms, read prayers for the dead and also give offerings to saints. A shroud was required too, and apart from all this, along with various other rituals, he also had to organize a feast for the community, give money to the poor and read from the Holy Koran.

The only way he could show devotion to his departed mother was by observing all the rituals. All his responsibilities towards his mother—temporal and spiritual—were coming to an end. Only her memories would be left behind to invoke at the time of difficulties. 'I could have achieved so much, if only God had given me the means. My condition is worse than the people around me.'

He started thinking about where he could get the money from. Now even Daudayal wouldn't give him a penny. 'I must at least visit him once. Who knows, may be his heart will melt after hearing my bitter story. He's a big man; if he chooses to be compassionate, a couple of hundred rupees will not even matter to him.'

After making up his mind he went to visit Daudayal. It wasn't easy for him to make the journey. How could he show his face to Daudayal and ask for more money? *Only three days have gone by since I promised him I would return the loan in a year's time. What will I say when I ask for two hundred more! If I had been in his place maybe even I wouldn't have given it. He may think that I'm not honest. What if he shuns me, or threatens me? What if he asks me on what grounds am I asking for more money? What will I say then? My hands are all the wealth I have. What else do I have? My house is of no value. The farms belong to the landowner; I have no claim left on them. I'm going in vain. He is sure to throw me out and whatever self-respect is left will be lost too.*

In spite of such a disheartening thought he plodded on ahead like a widow on her way to the police station to make an appeal.

Daudayal had returned from court and was as usual reprimanding the servants. 'Why haven't you sprinkled water at the gate or kept chairs in the veranda?' Meanwhile, Rehman inched towards him.

Daudayal was already annoyed, so he asked him with irritation, 'What are you here for? Why are you after my life? I don't have the time to talk right now.'

Rehman couldn't utter a word. He was so disappointed by the harsh words that he retraced his steps. *Hadn't I expected this? Didn't I know this would happen? I was foolish to hope.*

Daudayal became a little sympathetic. When Rehman had gone down the steps of the veranda Daudayal called him back and asked him kindly, 'Why have you come? Is it for some work?'

'No, master, I just dropped by to ask about your well-being.'

'There is a saying that a peasant never asks about someone's well-being without having an ulterior motive. What do you want, tell me.'

Rehman burst into tears. Daudayal guessed that his mother must have died. He asked, 'Rehman, has your mother passed away?'

'Yes, sir. It's been three days.'

'Don't cry, what good will it do? Calm down, this was God's will. Don't shed tears over her death. She died in front of your eyes, what can be better than that?'

'Sir, I have a request, but I can't gather the courage to voice it. My previous loan is still unpaid, how do I ask for more money? But Allah knows there is no possibility of getting money from anywhere else and my need is such that if I don't get the money for my purpose I will repent my whole life. I don't have the right to bother you. The rest is up to you. If you decide to give me the money then do bear in mind that you are throwing that money in a ditch. All I can say is that if I stay alive I will return each and every penny with interest. But do not refuse me at this hour.'

'Your loan has already added up to three hundred. In two years it will turn into seven hundred rupees. Do you realize that?'

'O Merciful! God willing, I will make a profit of five hundred by selling two acres land worth of sugar cane, and in two years I will be able to return every penny of yours.'

Daudayal once again gave him two hundred rupees. People familiar with his nature were surprised to see his leniency.

4

There are similarities between farming and the condition of an orphan child. If air and water are provided in required measures there will be a heap of grains. Without them even flourishing crops betray us like false friends. Crops need to survive hailstones and dike, famine and flood, locusts and weeds, termites and storms in order to reach the granary. And there is natural animosity between granaries and fire and electricity. If it is able to escape from all these enemies then it can be called a harvest; otherwise it might turn out to be a fatal judgement! Rehman toiled night and day. He didn't take a moment's rest. He forgot about his wife and children. His sugar cane grew so tall that if an elephant entered the farm it would have disappeared in it. The whole village was astonished. People said to him, 'Friend, you are very fortunate this time. You will definitely earn a minimum of seven hundred. All your problems will come to an end.' Rehman decided that the moment he got the money for the jaggery he would lay all of it at Daudayal's feet. Only if Daudayal himself returned four or five rupees would Rehman take it, otherwise he would spend the whole year on barley and bran.

But who can change the course of destiny? It was the month of December; Rehman was sitting on the boundary of his farm to guard it. He only had a coarse blanket to cover himself with, so he burned a few sugar cane leaves to keep himself warm. Suddenly, a gust of wind took a burning leaf towards the harvest. The farm caught fire. The villagers ran to smother the fire but the flames were like shooting stars which started from one end and quickly reached another. All measures to contain the fire failed. The whole farm burned to ashes and along with it Rehman's aspirations also shattered. The poor man was devastated. His heart sank. He lost all hope. It seemed as if a plate laden with food had been snatched away from him. When he returned home the anxiety about returning Daudayal's money again took hold of him. He wasn't bothered about himself or his children. A peasant is accustomed to hardship, to remain starved and unclothed. He was worried about the loan. 'The second year has begun. In a few days Daudayal's man will come to ask for the money. How will I show my face to him? I must again plead with him to give me a year's time. But then the amount will jump from seven hundred to nine hundred. And if he files a case I may have to return a thousand. Who is going to shower wealth on me in a year? He is such a considerate man; he lent me two hundred rupees so readily. Even my farm cannot be auctioned off. The oxen will barely fetch me four hundred. They aren't half as strong as they were. Now my honour is in the hands of God. I have done whatever I could.'

It was early in the morning. Rehman was standing at the boundary of his farm, witnessing the scene of his own destruction. He saw Daudayal's servant approaching him with a stick on his shoulder. He had been dreading the visit. 'God, only you can save me from this situation. What if he abuses me the moment he sees me? O God, where shall I hide!'

The servant approached Rehman and said, 'You don't want to return the money? The term ended yesterday. Don't you know the master! Even if one delays by a day he registers a case against that person. You will suffer terribly.'

Rehman started shivering. He said, 'You must have observed the condition of the farm.'

'I don't want to listen to any of your excuses. Fool someone else. Come quickly with seven hundred rupees.'

'My sugar cane crop has been gutted in the fire—all of it! Allah knows, this time I would have returned every penny.'

'I don't know all this. Only you are responsible for your sugar cane. Now, quick, follow me, Master has summoned you.'

The servant grabbed Rehman's arm and started dragging him away. The poor man wasn't even given enough time to tie a turban around his head.

5

They had covered around ten miles now. Rehman had not lifted his head even once. Every now and then he muttered, 'Allah, save me from this mess!' He had faith in Allah. Only this mantra kept him going for this long. Otherwise he would have fallen into pieces already. He had reached that level of despair where it was a kind of delusion rather than rationality that governed him.

Daudayal was standing at the gate. Rehman fell at his feet and said, 'I am in big trouble again. Allah knows that all my fortune has turned to dust.'

'Did all the sugar cane burn?'

'Master, have you heard about it already? It's as if somebody has swept the farm clean. The sugar cane crop had reached so high, kind master, that if the mishap hadn't occurred, I would have at least repaid the loan.'

'What do you intend to do now? Will you pay now or shall I file a suit?'

'Sir, you are my master, do as you please. I just know that I owe you money and must repay every penny. I don't care about myself. I promised you twice and both the times I failed to keep the promise. Now I won't make any promises.

Whenever I earn something I will keep it at your feet. I will toil, starve and save in whichever way I can to return your money.'

Daudayal smiled and said, 'What is your deepest desire right now?'

'The same, to return your money. Honestly. Allah knows.'

'Okay, then consider it repaid.'

'Master, how can this be true? If I don't pay you here I will have to repay you after my death in another world.'

'No, Rehman, do not worry about this any more. I was testing you.'

'Sir, don't say that. I don't want to die with this burden.'

'What kind of burden? You don't owe me anything. And even if you did, I have waived that, for this world and for the world after this too. Now you don't have to return anything to me. Actually I am only paying back whatever I owed you. *I* am *your* debtor, you are not my debtor. Your cow is still with me. She has given me at least eight hundred rupees' worth of milk. And also two calves as an additional profit. If you had given the cow to some brutes how would I have enjoyed this profit? You bore a loss of five rupees that time to sell the cow to me. I still remember your honesty. It isn't in my power to repay that favour. When you could bear the loss of five rupees in order to save the life of a cow despite being so poor, how can I, being a hundred times more affluent than you, be doing such a big service by waiving off four or five hundred rupees? Maybe you didn't intentionally do me a favour but it was a favour done to my rectitude. I gave you money for a just cause. Now you and I are even. Both your calves are here with me. If you like you can take them with you, they will help you till the soil. You are an honest and respectable person; I will always be ready to help you. In fact, tell me if you require money even now—you may take as much as you like."

Rehman felt as if an angel was sitting in front of him. If a man is generous, he appears like an angel; and if despicable, he seems like a devil. These are the two faces of a man. Rehman was so speechless that he could not even thank Daudayal. He somehow kept his tears in check and said, 'Sir, God will reward you for this kindness. I will consider myself your slave from this day onwards.'

'No, you are my friend.'

'No, sir, your slave.'

'The money a slave pays in order to free himself is called *muktidhan*. You have already paid that. Now never utter this word again in your life.'

Translated from the Hindi by Shradha Kabra

The Sacrifice

1

It is perhaps one's name that is most affected by one's social status. Ever since Mangru Thakur has become a constable he has been addressed as Mangal Singh. Now no one dare call him Mangru. And ever since Kallu Aheer has befriended Inspector Sahib and become the village headman, he has been called Kalka Deen. Now if someone calls him Kallu, he flies into a rage. Similarly, Harakh Chand Kurmi has now become Harkhu. Twenty years ago, his family had a sugar factory. They had several ploughs to cultivate land and had a flourishing business. But the import of foreign sugar had dealt such a blow to their business that the factory slowly disintegrated. The ploughs went out of use and the family business collapsed. Their land became barren and he became a broken man. This seventy-year-old man was once used to leaning against cushions on a charpoy and savouring coconut water. Now he carries manure in a basket on his head to earn a living.

Despite this, he retains an air of pride, maintains his sobriety, and his words carry dignity. He has remained unaffected by worldly affairs, untouched by the blows of destiny. Time leaves its stamp on noble men. Harkhu now possesses only five bighas of land, just a pair of oxen and one plough. Yet his advice is highly respected in panchayats and in matters of dispute. He does not mince his words; none in the village dare to disagree with him.

Never in his life did Harkhu take medicine though he had fallen ill at times. In the month of Kunwar, when the malaria epidemic spread, Harkhu was the first to be affected. But in a week or two he would recover without taking any medicine. So, when he fell ill this time, as usual, he didn't take medicine. But this time his fever carried the invitation of death. A week passed, then a fortnight, a whole month went by, but Harkhu could not leave his charpoy. Now he felt the need for medicine. His son, Girdhari, would sometimes make him drink the juice of neem stems or sometimes give him *garach* extract; at other times, Girdhari would feed him *gathborna* roots. But nothing seemed to work.

One day, Constable Mangal Singh went to inquire about Harkhu's health. Sitting on his broken charpoy, the poor man was chanting Lord Rama's name. Mangal Singh said, 'Baba, without medicine the illness won't go. Why not take quinine?'

Harkhu replied indifferently, 'Then you get it.'

The next day Kalka Deen went and said, 'Baba, take some pills for a few days. You don't have your old strength to get better without medication.'

To him, also, Harkhu replied indifferently, 'So, you bring it for me.'

But these were mere formalities devoid of any sympathy. No one bothered—neither Mangal Singh nor Kalka Deen, nor anyone else. Lying on the cot in his veranda, Harkhu would be lost in thought. If he saw Mangal Singh, he would ask, 'Bhaiya, didn't you get the medicine?' Mangal Singh simply ignored him. When he saw Kalka Deen he asked him the same question and Kalka Deen would look the other way. Either it never occurred to him that money was needed to buy medicines or money was more precious to him than life. Or perhaps he had no faith in medication and his philosophy was that when the illness had run its course it would vanish on its own. So, he never mentioned money and the medicine never came. His condition worsened. After five months of intense suffering, on the day of Holi, he passed away. Girdhari organized the funeral procession with great pomp and splendour. He performed all the rites with great resolve and fed Brahmins from several villages. The entire village was in mourning. No one celebrated the festival of Holi. Powder clouds of *abeer* and *gulal* did not rise, the drum beat was not heard, people did not drown themselves in the intoxicating bhang. Some cursed the old man for dying that day, others wished he had died a day or two later. But none were shameless enough to celebrate on the day of mourning. This was a village, not a city where no one bothers about the other, where a neighbour's cries do not reach us.

2

The villagers had their eyes set on Harkhu's fields. These fields comprised five bighas of fertile land, overlaid with compost, and wells situated nearby for irrigation. A mud bank formed the boundary. These fields yielded three crops a year. After Harkhu's death, there were numerous demands for his fields. While Girdhari was busy with the funeral rites, Lala Onkarnath was constantly hounded by the wealthy farmers of the village. Large sums of money were offered to Lalaji. While some offered to pay a year's rent in advance, others were ready to double the amount to draw up the documents of transfer. But Onkarnath would keep putting them off with one pretext or the other. He believed that Girdhari's father had worked those fields for twenty years and so Girdhari had the first right to it. Even if he paid a lesser amount as rent than others, Lalaji thought he should retain the land.

So, when Girdhari was through with the funeral rites and the month of Chait was about to get over, Onkarnath sent for him and asked, 'What are you thinking about the land?'

Girdhari burst into tears and said, 'My lord, these fields are my only hope. If I don't work them, what shall I do?'

'No, no. I don't ask you to give up the land. Harkhu tilled it for twenty years and never failed to pay. You're his son and you have a claim to this land. But don't you see the rates have gone up? You tilled at the rate of eight rupees per bigha, now I'm being offered ten rupees along with a commission of hundred rupees. As a concession, I'm willing to keep the old rate, but you must pay one hundred rupees as commission.'

'Sarkar, I can barely arrange for food for my family these days. From where shall I get such a huge sum? Whatever I had scrimped and saved till now has all gone in Dada's funeral. The harvest is yet to be reaped. With Dada's illness, even the rabi harvest has not been very good this time. From where am I going to get the money?'

'I know you're overburdened,' replied Onkarnath, 'and I'm aware you spent generously on the funeral. But you must understand that I cannot suffer any more losses. I've already conceded ten rupees a year to you. Isn't that enough?'

'Indeed, sarkar. You've been supporting us for so long; you've been most kind to us. Won't you be a little more kind? I'm a poor, humble servant of yours and if allowed to stay on this land, I'll serve you all my life. I can sell my oxen and offer you fifty rupees. That's about all I can do. The Lord has blessed you in many ways. Do me just this one favour!'

Onkarnath did not quite like Girdhari's refusal. He thought he had been more than considerate to Girdhari. No other zamindar would have been so lenient.

He said, 'You think we store all this money in our houses and lead a life of luxury. But only we know what we go through—donations here, offerings there, sometimes rewards, sometimes endowments. All these break our backbones. In addition, sometimes gifts have to be given. Whoever doesn't receive one, gets upset. For weeks, I'm worried about it. Then I have to make rounds of the bungalows, where I have to keep the orderlies and attendants in good humour. What my own children crave for but don't get, I offer to others. If I don't, life gets difficult. Then there are battalions of lawyers, sub-collectors, deputy sahibs arriving! If I'm not a good host to them, I lose face. Every year, a thousand odd rupees are spent on all this. From where do I get the money? To top it all, there are household expenses! I wish I could run away! This land is nothing but a liability! My whole life has been spent pleasing and entertaining officials! But for this land, I would have escaped somewhere, earned some money and lived in peace!

'We zamindars are God's deputies sent to oppress the poor. This is what we are born to do. We extort with one hand and reluctantly give away with the other. But you people think that we store it all in our houses. I'm being so generous but even after this if you are unhappy then it's your problem. Not a paisa less will I take! The month of Chait ends soon. If you can arrange for the money within a week, you can till the land. Otherwise, I'll make some other arrangement.'

3

Girdhari returned home, dejected and sad. It was beyond him to arrange for a hundred rupees. He wondered what he would do with the land if he sold his pair of oxen. If he tried selling his house, who would want to buy it? Also, it was an ancestral property. Though he owned a few trees, he wouldn't get more than twenty-five or thirty rupees for them. Were he to ask for a loan, who'd lend him money? He still owed the bania fifty rupees for the flour and ghee for the Brahmins' feast. There was no chance the bania would lend him another paisa. He possessed no jewellery or he would have sold it and got some money. The only thing he had was a necklace and that too was lying in the bania's custody. It had been with him for a year now and Girdhari had not been able to redeem it. He and his wife, Saubhagi, the lucky one, worried about it day and night but had failed to find a way out.

Girdhari could neither eat nor drink. At night, sleep eluded him. There was a constant load on his mind. The thought of losing his land consumed him. They had tilled this land for twenty long years, made it fertile, built its boundaries, and now someone else would reap the benefits.

His fields were his life. Every inch of that land was steeped in his blood; every speck of the soil was drenched in his sweat. The names he had given his fields flowed off his tongue as easily as the name of his three children. One was Chaubiso, another Bayiso; one he called Nalewala, the other Talaiyawala. A mention of these names conjured up the images of the fields in his mind. He talked about them as if they were alive, as if they were living beings. All his plans and all his dreams, all his fantasies and all his happiness, in fact all his expectations and his aims, grew out of these fields. He couldn't imagine life without them. And now he was on the verge of losing them. He would leave his house in extreme anguish and sit for hours on the edge of his field, weeping as if he were parting from it forever.

A whole week passed this way and Girdhari could not arrange for the money. On the eighth day, he came to know that Kalka Deen had given an advance of hundred rupees and purchased the land at ten rupees a bigha.

Girdhari heaved a deep sigh and his eyes filled with tears. The next moment, he called out his grandfather's name and wept inconsolably. There was wailing and weeping in the house where no fire was lit that day. It seemed as if Harkhu had died that very day and people were mourning his death.

4

But Saubhagi was not a woman to be content with her fate. In domestic discord, the bitterness and derision of her tongue would often come to the fore. She had great faith in the efficacy of this weapon and believed that it was very suitable in most situations. She didn't have the maturity to understand that it was beyond her power to remedy her misfortune and that resignation was the only resort available to her.

Filled with fury, she went to Kalka Deen's house and called his wife all kinds of names. 'Yesterday's pauper, today's prince! Wants to till my fields! I'll see who dares to take a plough to my land! I'll kill him! Arrogance for money! I'll tear it to pieces!'

Neighbours supported her. 'The truth is we don't want this competition amongst us. If God has given him wealth should he go around crushing the poor?'

Saubhagi thought she had won the battle. But it is the same wind which creates storms in the ocean that uproots trees too. While Saubhagi spent her time visiting neighbours where she bemoaned her situation, or fighting with Kalka Deen's wife, Girdhari, his heart filled with sadness, sat at his door wondering what he should do. *How can I go through life like this? Where would my children go for help?* The very thought of working as a labourer made his heart ache. After long years of a free and respectable life, living the life of a labourer seemed worse than death. He was master of a household and till now had been counted amongst the respectable people in the village. He had the right to voice his opinion on matters of the village. He didn't have the wealth but he certainly had a reputation. The village barber, carpenter, water carrier, priest and watchman looked up to him. Now, this respect was gone. Who'd seek his advice now, who'd come to his door for help? He had lost his social standing and the right to intervene in any matter. Now, he would have to earn a living as a slave to others. Now, who would prepare the oxen troughs late in the nights? Who would cut fodder for them? Those days, when he ploughed his land and sang, were gone forever. Those times, when he would sweat from head to toe and never feel tired, would never come again. He would never again exult in seeing his flourishing fields. The vast stores of grain would no longer be there to make him feel like an emperor. Who would now carry baskets from the granary? Gone was his granary, gone was his sustenance! This deserted place would now be home to gathering dust and stray dogs! Eyes would ache to see the oxen at this door; their hopeful eyes would never be seen again! This doorstep would lose its glory!

With these pitiful thoughts, tears fell from Girdhari's eyes. He stopped visiting anyone. He kept sitting at one place, filled with dejection and yearning. Some villagers, who were jealous of Kalka Deen, would come and sympathize with him but he remained reticent even with them. He felt he had fallen in people's eyes. If anyone told him that he had rashly spent on the funeral he did not like it. He did not regret what he had done. He would say, 'What destiny has ordained shall happen! At least I've cleared Dada's debts. His soul rests in peace now. In his lifetime, he fed others before eating himself. Should I have deprived him of funeral rites?'

Three months passed and the month of Asarh arrived. Dark clouds hung in the sky. Rain fell and the land turned green. Ponds and pits filled with water. Carpenters made rounds of farmers' houses to repair ploughs and make oxen yokes. Girdhari suffered in silence. Like an obsessed man, he moved in and out of his house. He would often look at his ploughs to see where repair was required. Once, while doing so, he was so deeply lost in thought that he ran to a carpenter and said, 'Rajju! My plough needs repair. Do it today!'

Rajju looked at him with surprise and went back to his work. Girdhari came to his senses almost as if he had been rudely awakened. His head fell in shame, tears flowed from his eyes. He returned home silently.

The village was bustling with activity. Someone looked for sunflower seeds; others purchased paddy seeds from the zamindar. While some discussed what to sow in the fields, others opined that it had rained too much and one should wait for a couple of days before sowing. Girdhari witnessed all this activity, heard all the discussions and felt helpless like a fish without water.

5

These days most of Girdhari's time was spent in taking care of his oxen. One evening, he stood scratching them when Mangal Singh arrived.

After exchanging pleasantries, Mangal said, 'How long are you going to keep these animals? Why don't you sell them?'

Sadly, Girdhari replied, 'I will, if I find a customer.'

'Sell them to me!'

Girdhari looked skywards and said, 'Take them if you like. What good are they to me now?'

These words had such sorrow and nostalgia in them. Till then, Girdhari had taken care of them in the faint hope of divine intervention. That day, the string of hope snapped. A bargain was struck. Girdhari had bought the animals for forty rupees; that day they were worth not less than eighty. Mangal Singh offered only fifty and Girdhari accepted the offer. Girdhari told himself that a little less or a little more hardly mattered when ruin stared him in the face. Mangal Singh got what his heart desired. He ran home and brought the money.

Sitting on Girdhari's cot, he counted the money while Girdhari stood next to his oxen, staring woefully at them—these were the animals that had earned for him, on whom all his hopes had rested! They were the light of his life, the essence of his dreams, and the good memories of his golden past! He felt as if his two hands were being torn away and that too for a paltry sum!

Finally, after Mangal Singh had counted and handed over the money, he untied the oxen and started to leave. Girdhari then put his head on the oxen's shoulders and wept inconsolably. Girdhari couldn't let go of his oxen like a weeping bride unable to leave her parental home; like a drowning man clutching on to the last straw. Saubhagi stood in the veranda and cried while their youngest son, only five years old, hit Mangal Singh with a stick.

Without eating anything, Girdhari lay on his cot that night but the next morning there was no sign of him. For the last several months he had stopped visiting people. Though suspicious, Saubhagi kept waiting for his return. When the clock struck eight and then nine, she began wailing. Many villagers gathered. Searches were conducted. But Girdhari was nowhere to be found. There was a flicker of hope and so there was no breaking of bangles to mourn widowhood. Evening had set in and darkness spread. Saubhagi lit a lamp and kept it beside Girdhari's charpoy. Her eyes were fixed on the door, waiting. Her infant daughter slept in her lap while her young son was throwing a tantrum, demanding his Dada's return. Saubhagi suddenly heard footsteps and her heart burst with happiness. She ran towards the door but the charpoy was empty. She peeped outside while her heart throbbed. She saw Girdhari standing by the trough, head bowed and crying. Saubhagi spoke up, 'Come inside. What are you doing standing there? We've been so worried right through the day!' Saying this she moved quickly towards him, but he did not respond. He stepped backwards after some time and vanished into thin air. Saubhagi let out a loud shriek and fell down, unconscious.

The next day, before the break of dawn, Kalka Deen reached his newly acquired field with his plough. It was still a little dark. He was tying the oxen to the plough when suddenly he saw Girdhari standing at the boundary of the field. He was wearing the same jacket and turban. His head was bowed. Kalka Deen exclaimed, 'Arré Girdhari! What a man you are! Poor Saubhagi is worrying about you and you're here! Where have you been?'

Saying this, he left his oxen and walked towards Girdhari. But Girdhari stepped back and jumped into the well behind him. Kalka Deen screamed loudly. Throwing aside his plough, he ran frantically homewards.

But he did not say a word to his workers. The next day, he sent one of his workers, Jheengur, to the field. Evening set in, men and cattle returned home but Jheengur did not return. Night came but there was no sign of him. Worried, Kalka Deen went to the field along with some villagers. He saw the oxen lying on one side and Jheengur lying unconscious on the other. They shook him, called out his name, but he remained unconscious. A few men carried him back home. The hooves of the oxen were found to be bleeding. People realized immediately that when Jheengur had fainted the animals must have struggled to break free. As the oxen were yoked together, their struggle must have injured their hooves. Jheengur was hysterical the entire night. He regained consciousness only in the morning. He told them that he had seen Girdhari standing near the east-side well; that he had called out to him several times but Girdhari didn't respond. When he moved towards Girdhari, the latter simply jumped into the well. He could not recollect what had happened thereafter. Word spread through the entire village and there was all sorts of speculation. From that day, Kalka Deen could never gather the courage to enter the field. After dusk, no one walked on that path.

6

Today, it's been six months since the incident. Girdhari's eldest son now works in a brick kiln and earns ten to twelve annas every day. He wears a shirt and English shoes. At home, curry is cooked twice a day, and they can now afford wheat and rice instead of millet. But he has lost his status in the village. He is just another labourer.

Saubhagi's sharp tongue and arrogance are gone. Her fire has turned to ashes, it can burn no one. Even a weak breeze can extinguish her. She is an outsider in the village, a pariah dog, not seen in panchayats any more. She visits no one, and no one invites her. Hopes have perished but memories linger as Saubhagi is now a figure of helplessness. Girdhari's funeral rites have also not been completed. Kalka Deen has forsaken his land because Girdhari's restless spirit haunts the fields. It does not harm anyone, and seems to derive comfort from watching the fields. Onkarnath has often tried to sell the land but villagers are too scared to even look in that direction.

Translated from the Urdu by M. Asaduddin

The Roaming Monkey

1

Jeevan Das was a poor juggler. He earned his living through the acrobatics of his monkey, Mannu. Both he and his wife, Budhiya, loved him deeply. Since they were childless, Mannu alone was the object of their love. Both of them fed him with their own hands and put him to sleep in bed like a child. Nothing was dearer to them than Mannu.

Once, Jeevan Das brought a ball for him, which Mannu played with in the courtyard. There was an earthen bowl for his food, a sack cloth for sleeping and a blanket rag for covering his body. There was also a rope hanging from the roof for his jumps. Mannu deeply cherished these things. He wouldn't eat until something was put in his bowl. His sack cloth and his blanket rag were dearer to him than a shawl or a mattress. He spent his days happily. Every morning, he ate his chapattis and went with Jeevan Das to perform his acrobatic feats. His skill at acting captivated the spectators. Grabbing a stick, he would walk like an old man, sit in a position of prayer, make the gesture of a tilak on his forehead and hold pages from the scriptures in his hand and pretend to read them. He would beat the drum and pretend to sing in such an endearing way that the spectators split their sides with laughter. When the spectacle got over, he saluted everyone and touched people's feet to beg money from them. Mannu's bowl would fill with coins. After this, if someone fed Mannu a guava, someone else threw a piece of sweet before him. Boys never got tired of watching him. They would run to their houses to fetch pieces of bread to feed him. Mannu was the main entertainer for the people of the mohalla. As long as he was in the house, someone or the other would come to play with him. The street vendors would give him something to eat. If any of them tried to go past him without giving him anything, he touched their feet and extracted his share from them, as he stayed in the house free, without being tied. The only creatures Mannu had a distaste for were dogs. No dog dared pass by his house. If any did, Mannu served him one or two tight slaps. This was another reason for his popularity. On some days, when Budhiya slept in the sun, Mannu would stand near her head and pick out lice from her hair. Sometimes Budhiya sang for him. Mannu followed her wherever she went. Surely even a mother and her son weren't so attached to each other.

2

One day, Mannu felt like eating some fruits. Now, there were fruits to eat, but the pleasure of climbing up trees and hanging from the branches, eating some and throwing away others was something else. Monkeys are usually entertaining. Mannu was a little more so. So far, he had never been caught or beaten. Climbing up trees and eating fruits came to him naturally. He didn't know that even objects in nature belonged to someone or the other. Why, people exerted claims on even water, air and light, never mind orchards and gardens. When Jeevan Das returned at noon after the show, Mannu made his escape. He usually roamed around the mohalla, so no one suspected him of going anywhere else. He roamed the streets, jumped over the roofing tiles and finally reached an orchard. He saw that the trees there were laden with fruits. He was delighted to see gooseberries, jackfruits, litchis, mangoes and papayas hanging from the trees. It was as though the trees were beckoning him to come and feed on the fruits as much as he wanted. He leapt on a wall and then leapt up a tree. He ate some mangoes and then moved on to litchis and threw the stones around. Then he climbed up the highest branch of another tree and began to shake the branches. The ground filled up with ripe mangoes. The noise woke up the gardener from his siesta. The moment he sighted Mannu, he began to throw stones at him. These stones didn't reach him, and the ones that did he escaped by ducking or manoeuvring his body cleverly. He even frightened the gardener by making faces at him and baring his teeth, threatening to bite him. The gardener backed off but came back again with a fresh supply of stones. The boys of the mohalla gathered around to see the fun and raised a racket:

> Hey, monkey, *loyelaaye*,
> We shall pull out your hairs *toyetaaye*,
> Hey monkey, your face is red,
> And your cheeks are shrunken.

His maternal grandmother is dead,
While the moustached-one has a broken leg.

Mannu was enjoying the fun and frolic. He ate half the fruits
and threw the rest down, which the boys picked up promptly.
They clapped their hands and sang:

Bandar Mamu, can you say,
Where do you stay?

When the gardener saw that the situation couldn't be
brought under control, he went and informed his master.
This gentleman was an official in the police department.
The moment he heard the news, he lost his temper. *What
audacity! How dare this monkey come to my orchard and raise
such a racket. I pay the rent of the bungalow, not him. I have
crushed many who have stepped in my way—even the newspaper
people are scared of me! And I'm being challenged by a monkey!*
He picked up his gun and went to the orchard, where he saw
Mannu shaking a tree vigorously. Furious, he aimed his gun
at Mannu. The monkey lost his wits at the sight of the gun.
No one had ever aimed a gun at him. However, he had heard
the sound of the gun and seen birds killed following gunshots.
Even if he hadn't seen it before, it was natural for him to be
scared at the sight of the gun. His animal instincts made him
stay clear of his enemies. But it was as though Mannu's feet
were paralysed. He couldn't even jump to another tree. He
stayed on the same branch quietly. The owner of the orchard
liked Mannu's ways and he suddenly took pity on him. He
sent the gardener to catch Mannu and bring him over to him.
The gardener was scared, but he was familiar with his master's

anger. He climbed up the tree quietly, tied the monkey with a rope and brought him down.

Mannu was tied to a pole in the corridor of the bungalow. He lost his spirit. He stayed there till late evening, whining. At sundown, a servant came and threw a fistful of grams before him. Mannu became acutely aware of the change in his situation. There was no blanket, and no sackcloth. He was lying on the bare floor and whining. He didn't even touch the grams. He was regretting his little adventure now, and kept thinking about the juggler. *The poor fellow must be wandering around, searching for me. The juggler's wife must be calling my name, holding pieces of bread and milk in her hand. Where have I landed?* He kept waking through the night, and circled the pole. Tommy, the master's dog, barked at him every now and then to frighten him. Mannu felt extreme anger towards him and wanted to hit him hard. But the dog didn't come close. He only kept barking from a distance.

When the night turned into dawn, the master came and gave Mannu a few tight slaps. 'Swine! Spoiled my sleep at night by yelping constantly. I couldn't close my eyes even for a second. If you create a racket today, I'll shoot you.' Saying this, he left. Now it was the turn of the naughty boys. Some of them were from the mohalla, some of them were from outside. Some made faces at Mannu, some threw stones at him, while others beckoned him with sweets. No one came to his rescue, no one felt any pity for him. He tried every possible method to save himself, but he couldn't escape. He saluted the boys, showed them his posture of pray and worship, and the only reward he got from the boys was more teasing. That day no one even threw grams at him. Even if they did, he was not in a position to eat. Sorrow had dulled his urge for eating.

The juggler reached the sahib's house in the evening, after much inquiry. When Mannu saw him, he leapt with such impatience it almost seemed as if he would break the shackles and bring down the pillar. The juggler hugged Mannu and said to the sahib, 'Huzoor, he is a mere animal. Even men make mistakes. Give me whatever punishment that you want, but please spare him. Master, he is the only source of my livelihood. My wife and I will starve to death without him. We have reared him like our own child. My wife hasn't had any food since he ran away. Please have some mercy, Master. May you be prosperous forever, may you achieve a higher status, may your pens become mightier and may your cases be liquidated. You are the good son of your father, may you always remain strong. May your rivals be ruined.' But the sahib remained unmoved. He berated the juggler. 'Shut up, you rogue, you have annoyed me with your endless talking. First you let your monkey ruin my orchard, and then you come here to placate me with your glib tongue! Just go and see how many fruits he has spoiled. If you want to take him with you, then compensate my losses with ten rupees, otherwise be on your way without a word. He will die here with his limbs tied until someone pays the penalty and takes him away.'

The juggler left in despair. Where on earth could he manage to get the ten rupees from? He told Budhiya about the situation. Budhiya was more convinced about her ability to elicit sympathy. She said, 'I know you! You must have given him a tongue-lashing. You must use your words carefully while talking to these masters. Only then will they be pleased. Come with me, watch me bring him back.' She tied all of Mannu's belongings in a bundle and went to the sahib along with her husband. This time Mannu jumped so forcefully that the pillar actually shook. Budhiya said, 'Master, we've come to beg at your door. Please give this monkey to us as charity.'

The sahib replied, 'I consider charity to be a sin.'

The juggler's wife said, 'We roam around villages and towns. We will sing your praises.'

'I don't care for anyone singing my praises.'

'God will reward you for this.'

'I know nothing about God.'

'My lord, forgiveness is a great virtue.'

'To me, punishment has great virtue.'

'My lord, you're our master. You have to do justice to us. Please don't take the lives of two individuals for a few fruits. It is justice which makes a man great.'

'My greatness doesn't lie in forgiveness and justice. It is not my duty to ensure justice. My work is to enjoy myself.'

None of Budhiya's arguments had any effect on this vain person. Disheartened, she said, 'Sir, show some kindness and let us keep these things near the monkey. He is attached to them.'

'I've no place here to keep your dirty rags.'

The juggler and his wife left in utter despair.

3

When Tommy saw that Mannu was a harmless creature he grew bolder. He moved closer to Mannu, growling. Mannu leapt at him, catching his ears, and gave him such tight slaps that the dog was dumbfounded. Hearing his screams, the master came out of his room and gave Mannu several kicks. He ordered his servants not to give any food to the rogue monkey for three days.

It was a coincidence that the manager of a circus company visited the master that day to seek his permission to hold shows. When he saw Mannu sitting tearfully, tied to a pole, he came close and smiled at him. Mannu jumped up, fell at his feet and began to salute him. The manager understood that he was domesticated. He needed a monkey for his circus. He talked to the master, gave him a fair price and took Mannu with him. However, Mannu soon realized that he had now landed up in a worse place. The manager gave him to a servant who was in charge of the monkeys. The servant was a very cruel and crude person. There were several monkeys in his care. Each one of them was in terrible pain. The keeper would eat up all the food meant for the monkeys. The other monkeys didn't welcome Mannu into their midst. His coming created a commotion among them. If the keeper hadn't separated them, they would've made mincemeat of him. Mannu had to learn new acts now—riding a bicycle, climbing on to a running horse and standing on it with his two hind legs, walking on a fine rope and other such scary activities. He was often subjected to beating so he could learn these things properly. If he made the slightest mistake, he was caned on the back. Even more painful was the fact that he was confined to a cell throughout the day so that no one could see him. Mannu had performed acrobatics even when he lived with the juggler, but there was great difference between the two lives. The juggler had loved him, talked to him endearingly. But in this place, he was a prisoner, subjected to beatings and cruelty. He was taking time to learn the new skills because he was still constantly thinking about running away to Jeevan Das. Every day, he waited for an opportunity to run away but the animals were kept under strict surveillance in the circus. They didn't even get fresh air, let alone the smallest opportunity to run away. Everyone was busy making him work; no one cared for his meals. Mannu had escaped the master's bungalow quickly enough but he had now spent three months in this prison. His health worsened, and he was completely miserable. He had to work, whether he wanted or not. The owner of the circus only wanted to earn money; he didn't care if Mannu lived or died.

One day, the circus tent caught fire. All the workers in the circus were gamblers. They would gamble, drink liquor and fight amongst themselves throughout the day. Amidst this mess, the gas pipes exploded suddenly. A commotion ensued. The spectators ran for their lives. The employees of the company started clamouring for their belongings. No one bothered about the animals. There were two lions, many cheetahs, one elephant and a bear. The number of dogs, horses and monkeys was much more. The company had never even cared for the lives of its employees in its quest for earning money. The animals were taken off their tethers only for their performances. When the fire broke out, they all ran away. Mannu, too, made his escape. He didn't even look back to see whether the tent had burnt completely or if it was still safe.

Mannu went straight to Jeevan Das's house. But the door was closed. He climbed up on the roofing tiles and made his way inside the house. But, there was no one inside. The place where he slept, which was usually plastered clean with cow dung by Budhiya, was now covered with grass. The wood on which he would climb up and jump around had been consumed by termites. The people of the mohalla recognized him immediately. A noise broke out—'Mannu has come, Mannu has come.'

Mannu would go to the house every day in the evening and lie down on his old spot. He would roam around the mohalla throughout the day and only ate if someone gave him anything. He never touched anyone's belongings. He still hoped to meet his old master somewhere in the area. The pitiable sound of his whining could be heard in the nights. Everybody was moved to tears by his plight.

Several months passed in this manner. One day, Mannu was sitting in the street when he heard some boys making a commotion. He saw an old woman, her head uncovered and her hair dishevelled. She was unclothed save for the rags wrapped around her waist. Like a ghost, she walked towards him. The boys behind her were pelting stones at her, shouting, 'Mad Naani, Mad Naani' at her and clapping their hands as they followed her. Every now and then she would stop and tell the boys, 'I'm not insane. Why are you calling me mad?' Finally, she sat on the ground and said, 'Tell me, why do you call me mad?' She wasn't even a bit angry with the boys. She neither cried nor smiled. She kept quiet even when the stones hit her.

One of the boys asked, 'Why don't you wear clothes? What else is this if not madness?'

The old woman replied, 'Clothes are worn for protection against the cold in the winter season. It's summer these days.'

The boy asked again, 'Aren't you ashamed of yourself?'

The old woman answered, 'What is it that you call shame? There are so many ascetics who remain naked all their lives. Why don't you hit them with stones?'

The boy said, 'They are men.'

The old woman asked, 'Is shame the preserve of only women? Shouldn't men feel this shame?'

'You eat whatever is thrown at you. Only a mad person does that,' the boy persisted.

'What is so mad about it? If one feels hungry, one has to fill one's belly.'

'You've no sense of discrimination. Don't you feel repelled by these things?'

'I don't know what repulsion is. Nothing repels me now.'

'Everyone is repelled by something or the other. Shall I explain to you what repulsion is?'

Another boy piped in, 'Why do you throw away the money people give you? If someone offers you clothes, you don't take them. Why shouldn't we call you mad?'

'What should I do with money or clothes?'

'You need them. Everyone lusts for money.'

'What is lust, son? I've forgotten it.'

'That is why we call you mad granny. You've no lust, no repulsion, no shame, no sense of discrimination. That's why you're called mad.'

'Then so be it. Let me be a mad woman.'

'Why don't you feel anger?'

'I don't know, son. I just don't feel angry at anything. Do people really feel angry? I've forgotten how to.'

At this, several boys broke out into a clamour—'Mad woman, mad woman'—but the old woman quietly proceeded on her way. When she came close, Mannu recognized her. It was Budhiya. He threw himself at her feet. A startled Budhiya looked down at him, and then clutched him to her chest.

4

As soon as she took Mannu in her lap, Budhiya realized that she was naked. Overcome by shame, she sat down and called out to a boy. 'Son, could you give me something to wear?'

'Didn't you say that you'd lost your sense of shame?'

'No, son. Now I've got it back. I don't know what had happened to me.'

When the boys again shouted 'Mad woman, mad woman,' she started hitting them with stones. She even ran after them.

One of the boys asked, 'A moment ago, you knew nothing about anger. So why on earth are you getting furious now?'

'I don't know why I am getting angry now. If anyone calls me mad again, I'll have him bitten by the monkey.'

One of the boys came running with a tattered rag. The old woman wore it. She also arranged her hair. The insanity that glowed on her face earlier was replaced by the sombre glow of reflection. Crying, she said to Mannu, 'Oh, son, where had you gone? It has been such a long time . . . didn't you care about us? Your master passed away longing for you. I begged in order to fill my belly. The house was reduced to shambles. When you were here, I cared about food, clothes, jewellery and the house. But all my desires vanished as soon as you went away. I was troubled by hunger, but nothing else mattered for me in this world. My eyes didn't shed any tears even when your master died. He was groaning with pain while lying on the cot, but my heart had turned into stone. Forget getting medicines for him, I didn't even care to stand beside his bed. I would think "Who is he?" Now when I remember all those things and the state which I was in, I have to admit that I had indeed become insane and it was only right that the boys should call me "Mad Naani".'

Budhiya went with Mannu to a garden outside the town. She lived in that garden under a tree. There was only some straw there for her to lie on. There was no other object necessary for survival.

From that day onwards, Mannu began to live with Budhiya. He'd leave the shelter in the morning and return home with some vegetables and bread that he'd earned showing off his acrobatics or simply begging. Even if Budhiya had a son, he wouldn't have showed his mother the kind of love that Mannu showed. People were delighted by his acts and gave him money in return for the entertainment. Budhiya bought food from the market with this money.

People were amazed by Mannu's deep love for Budhiya. They declared that Mannu was not a monkey but a deity.

Translated from the Hindi by M. Asaduddin

Reincarnation

1

Material prosperity rarely comes to gentlemen. Ramtahal, who enjoyed a life of luxury, was dissipated and morally degraded. He was a cunning man, good at extracting interest out of loaned money and always on the winning side in legal transactions. His wealth kept increasing. Everyone was his prey. On the other hand, his younger brother, Shivtahal, was religious, devout, and helpful. His wealth kept decreasing. There were always at least two or three guests hovering at his doorstep. His elder brother had a lot of clout in the neighbourhood. Those who belonged to the lower castes followed his orders promptly. His house was repaired free of cost. Those indebted to him came with offerings of all kinds. For instance, some from the Kunjre caste would get *saag-bhaji*, while the Goalas would give him milk—that also one and a half times the quantity of what one would get at the market price. The younger brother had no such clout. Sadhus and mendicants would be his visitors; they would eat their fill in his house and go on their way. If he gave money to people, it was not with the intention of earning interest, but to help them out in their hour of need. He could not demand his own money from his debtors forcefully, lest he hurt their sentiments.

In this manner quite a few years went by. Whatever inheritance Shivtahal possessed was squandered in his pursuit of salvation. Much of his money sank. Ramtahal, on the contrary, got a new house built. He also opened a shop for doing business in gold and silver. He bought some land too and started farming.

Shivtahal was now worried. How could he live like this? He did not have money to generate an income. He did not possess the skills that help one earn a living without wealth. He didn't even have the courage to borrow money from anyone. How would he repay them if he ran into losses? He couldn't even look for employment under anyone because then the family honour would be at stake. Finally, finding no other recourse, he went to his elder brother and said, 'Brother, now you have to take the responsibility of looking after me and my family. Where else can I go seeking refuge?'

Ramtahal said, 'You don't have anything to worry about. You have not squandered your money in evil deeds. Whatever you have done has only boosted the honour of our family. I am cunning; I know how to trick the world. You are a simple man. Others have cheated you. This is your house too. You can collect the revenues from the lands I have bought, and look after the farming there. Whatever you spend each month, come and take it from me. But I have one condition. I won't spend a single penny on sadhus and mendicants. And I wouldn't like you to speak ill of me.'

Shivtahal, overcome with emotion, said, 'Brother, I have surely sinned by always speaking ill of you; my apologies. If you ever hear me speak ill of you again, give me whatever punishment you deem fit. I have one request to make, though. Do ensure that your wife stops chastising me for whatever good or bad I have done so far.'

Ramtahal said, 'If ever again I hear her speak ill of you, I will pull out her tongue.'

2

Ramtahal's lands were some twenty-five miles away from the town. A temporary house had been built there. The bullocks, the cart and all the farming implements were kept there. Shivtahal gave his house to his brother and went to live in the village with his children. He started working in earnest there. The farmhands were alerted. The fruits of labour were evident. In the first year itself, the farm produce doubled and expenses were reduced by half.

But how does one change one's nature? Though it was not like before, one or two characters would still come to visit Shivtahal after hearing of his success. Shivtahal was forced to look after them. Of course, he concealed these incidents from his brother, so that Ramtahal in his annoyance wouldn't put an end to this source of livelihood. The result was that Shivtahal was compelled to sell vegetables, fodder, oil cakes and other such things on the sly. To make up for this, he extracted more work from the labourers and he exerted himself too. He ignored the heat and cold, and even the rains completely. But the problem was he had not worked this hard ever before. His health deteriorated. The food he ate was not wholesome either. Nor did he maintain any proper hours.

Sometimes he would eat at midday, sometimes in the late afternoon. When thirsty, he would go straight to the pond. Weakness indicated the onset of disease. He soon fell ill. No medicine was available in the village. The food he was eating was not suitable for his condition. He began to fall sick; the fever now caught his spleen and in six months' time he passed away.

Ramtahal was depressed by the news. In the past three years, he had not bought even a paisa's worth of grains. Jaggery, butter, fodder for animals, fuel in the form of cow-dung cakes . . . everything came from the village. Overcome by remorse, he regretted being so negligent about his brother's treatment, drowned as he was in his own selfish pursuits. But how was he to know that the fever could take such a fatal turn? Had he realized the seriousness of the situation, he would have definitely taken care of Shivtahal's medical treatment. If this was God's will, how could he have changed anything?

3

Now there was no one to look after the lands. Ramtahal had tasted the pleasure of farming. His wayward lifestyle had affected *his* health too. He now wanted to live in the salubrious climate of the village. He decided to move to the village and work on the land. He delegated his business in the city to his son, who had grown up by now.

In the village he devoted all his time and energy to looking after the cows. He had one large cow that hailed from the banks of the Yamuna. He had bought her some years ago with great enthusiasm. She yielded a lot of milk and was so simple that even when children grabbed her horns, she did not protest. At that time she was pregnant. Ramtahal loved her dearly. He would look after her day and night, sometimes stroking her back, sometimes feeding her fodder—all with his own hands. Many offered more than double her price but Ramtahal did not sell her. When the cow gave birth, Ramtahal celebrated the occasion with a lot of fanfare; many Brahmins were fed on the day. The festivities continued for several days. The calf was named Jawahir. An astrologer was called to draw his birth chart. According to him the calf was very intelligent, auspicious and devoted to him. Only in the sixth year there was a chance of some misfortune. If he somehow managed to sail through that then he would lead a happy life till the very end.

The calf was milk white. A red tilak was painted on his forehead. His eyes were dark. His features were beautiful and his limbs well shaped. He kept mooing the entire day. Ramtahal was delighted by his pranks. The calf became so fond of him that he would follow him around like a dog. Jawahir would stand beside him while he was attending to his clients in the mornings and evenings and keep licking him all over. When Ramtahal's hands stroked his back with affection, his tail would go erect and his eyes would dance with joy. Ramtahal, too, was so fond of him that unless he sat on his charpoy to play with the calf, he found no taste in his food. He would often hug him and pet him. He got a silver necklace specially made for him, decked him with silk flowers and even got him silver anklets. He appointed a man to give the calf a bath every day and also dust him regularly. If Ramtahal was seen seated on a horse so he could visit neighbouring villages, Jawahir would start lowing and rush towards him to lick his feet. This father-and-son relationship between a man and an animal was so unique that everybody was surprised by it.

4

Jawahir was now two and a half years old. Ramtahal thought of putting him to work. He had grown from a calf to a bull. He had a round hump, a well-shaped body, powerful muscles, a broad chest and a joyful stride. There was no bull as wonderful as him in the neighbourhood. It was difficult to get another like him. When Jawahir was yoked with another bull, it was obvious that the pair did not match. People said that though the owner had spent a lot of money he could not find one even remotely equal to Jawahir! They were as different as the light of an electric lamp and that of an oil lamp.

It was curious that Jawahir would not lift his foot when the cart driver hollered. He simply shook his neck. But when Ramtahal took the reins and coaxed him affectionately, 'Come on, son,' Jawahir would fly off with the cart. He would cover several miles in one breath without stopping anywhere. Even horses were unable to match him.

One evening, when Ramtahal was chasing away flies as Jawahir fed on oil cakes and husk, a wandering mendicant arrived and stood at the doorstep. Ramtahal welcomed him with utmost humility. 'Why stand there? Do come in.'

The mendicant said, 'I'm just watching this bull. I have never seen such a handsome one.'

'He is from this house.'

'He is a living God.' He then started kissing Jawahir's hooves.

Ramtahal asked, 'Where do you hail from? Do take some rest here. I will be obliged.'

'No, my dear man, pardon me. I have to catch a train for some important work. I will be delayed if I wait the night.'

'Will I meet you again?'

'Yes, definitely, after three years of pilgrimage, I will be back this way. I will spend the night here then. You are a blessed soul—you have the opportunity to serve a Nandi like this. Don't consider him an animal. He is some great soul born in this form. Do not ever hurt him. Do not ever hit him, even by mistake.'

The mendicant then touched Jawahir's hoof again and went on his way.

5

From that day on, Jawahir got even better treatment. From an animal he graduated to a God. Ramtahal first fed him from the kitchen and then had his own meal. First thing in the morning he visited him as one does a sacred shrine. He went so far as to desist from even yoking him to the cart. But when Ramtahal had to go somewhere and was forced to take out the cart, Jawahir became eager to be yoked to it; in excitement he would keep nodding his head, making it difficult for Ramtahal to do anything else. A few times, when he took the other pair to draw the cart, it upset Jawahir so much that he refused to eat anything the whole day. That is why Ramtahal refrained from going anywhere unless it was an emergency.

Seeing Ramtahal's faith, the other villagers too started feeding grains to Jawahir. Many would visit him in the morning to make their offerings.

Three years went by in this manner. Now Jawahir was in his sixth year.

Ramtahal remembered what the astrologer had said. He was afraid that the prediction would come true. He got many books on veterinary science and started reading them. He met a vet and procured some medicines too. He got Jawahir vaccinated. Fearing that the servants might give him the wrong fodder, or water that was not clean, he took on the entire responsibility of looking after Jawahir. The shed was cemented so that harmful germs or insects were kept away. Every day he would wash the place thoroughly.

It was evening. Ramtahal was standing beside Jawahir, feeding him from a tumbler. Suddenly the mendicant who had visited him three years ago arrived. Ramtahal recognized him immediately. After greeting the mendicant, he inquired about his well-being and then went in to arrange a meal. All of a sudden Jawahir belched loudly and fell to the ground. Ramtahal was at his side in a moment. Jawahir's eyes glazed over. He looked at Ramtahal with love and then became still.

Scared, Ramtahal went to get the medicines. He could not understand what had happened. When he reached with the medicines, he found that Jawahir was already dead.

Ramtahal hadn't felt so much sorrow even when his younger brother had died. He would keep running to the bull's side and hold him close, crying his heart out, even though people tried to stop him.

Ramtahal cried through the whole night. Jawahir's memory kept surfacing in his mind. Sorrow weighed heavily on him, gripping him at intervals.

Early the next morning Jawahir's body had to be disposed of but Ramtahal did not allow the tanners to come and take him away as per the custom in the village. He cremated the bull in accordance with the scriptures, lighting the pyre himself. He religiously performed all the rituals associated with death. He served meals to the Brahmins of the village on the thirteenth day. The mendicant who had come to him was still by his side—Ramtahal wouldn't let him go. The mendicant's words helped him calm down a little.

6

One day he asked the mendicant, 'Mahatmaji, I still don't understand—what ailed Jawahir? The astrologer had predicted that his sixth year would not go well. But I have not seen any animal die like this. You are a yogi; can you solve this riddle?'

The mendicant said, 'I can make some sense of it.'

'Do tell me. My mind is not at peace.'

'In his past life, he must have been an honest, helpful and deeply religious man. He had spent all his money on good deeds in the name of religion. Was there any relative of yours who had been like this?'

'Yes, sir, there was one.'

'He must have cheated you, betrayed your trust. You must have entrusted him with some work, and he used your money to serve followers of religion like sadhus and mendicants on the sly.'

'He was such a simple-minded, honest fellow. The thought of cheating anyone wouldn't even have crossed his mind.'

'But he did betray your trust. Not out of self-interest but to serve others. It is still cheating.'

'Circumstances probably swayed him from the path of duty.'

'Yes, it is so. It must have been ascertained that he deserved a place in heaven, but he had to atone for betraying somebody's trust. Whatever money he had cheated you out of had to be paid back, so he was born here as an animal in this birth. It was certain that in six years' time he would be able to atone for the sin he'd committed. He stayed with you to fulfil that time period. Once the period was over, his soul left his body to embark on the eternal journey.'

The mendicant left the next day. A great change came over Ramtahal. His attitude to life changed completely. His heart was filled with kindness and sensitivity. He started thinking that if such a devout man like his brother had to undergo punishment for one mistake, then what must lie awaiting *him* for all *his* misdeeds! He could never drive this thought away from his mind.

Translated from the Hindi by Anuradha Ghosh

Turf War

1

By appearance Tommy looked quite hefty; when he barked he could burst people's eardrums. His gait was such that on dark nights people mistook him for a donkey, but his valour was proven in the battlefield. A couple of times when the lumpen elements in the market offered him a challenge, he descended on the arena to smash their pride, and eyewitnesses say that as long as he fought, he fought strongly, his tail dealing more blows than his nails or teeth. It couldn't be said with certainty who had won the fight in the end but since the other party had to ask for reinforcements, then, according to the laws of the battlefield, it seemed reasonable that the victory trophy should go to Tommy. On that occasion, Tommy acted pragmatically and bared his teeth, which was a requirement for truce. But since then he had stopped engaging with such unprincipled adversaries.

Tommy was peace-loving, but the number of his enemies increased by the day. His peers were jealous of him because he was lean instead of roly-poly. The troop in the market envied him because he did not allow any bones to escape his grip.

He woke up early in the morning and licked all that was left
over in the leaf plates in front of the sweetshop and chewed
all the bones left in front of the abattoir. Thus, surrounded
by such a large number of enemies, Tommy's life was full of
difficulties. Months would pass till he came by a meal that
would fill his belly. Several times he had had such a longing
for a heavy meal that he had filled his belly with dubious
stuff, and the consequences had been grave. For several days,
he suffered from a severe ache, not in his stomach but in his
back. Having learnt his lesson he began to follow the path of
restraint. Though restrained, his longing did not stop. He
wanted to go to a place filled with prey—there should be
hare, antelopes and sheep grazing in the field with no one
to look after them, and no rivals to offer him a fight. There
should be shady trees for his rest and sweet river water to slake
his thirst. He would kill them at his will, have his meal and go
into deep sleep. Everyone around that place would be afraid
of him and accept him as their king. Slowly, he would be so
powerful that no jealous rival would have the courage to step
into his area. One day, lost in such sweet dreams, Tommy
had left the main road and was passing through a lane when
he had an encounter with a gentleman dog. Tommy wanted
to walk past him, but the gentleman was not as peace-loving
as Tommy. He pounced on Tommy and caught him by his
snout. Tommy fell at his feet and cringed, 'For God's sake
let me go. I take this oath that I won't step here again. It
was my ill luck that I had entered your area.' But that cruel
and vain creature did not show him the slightest mercy.
Defeated, Tommy began to whine like a donkey. Hearing
this commotion, several leaders of the mohalla gathered
there, but instead of showing mercy to the oppressed they

began to cut their teeth on him. Such unjust treatment broke Tommy's heart. He left the scene with his life. The cruel animals chased him for a long distance. There was a river before him. Tommy jumped into the river to save his life.

It is said that every dog has his day. Tommy's day came when he jumped into the river. He had jumped into it to save his life, but he came upon a pearl. Swimming across the river he reached the other bank, and saw his long-cherished dream taking shape into reality.

2

It was a huge field. As far as the eyes could see, it was all lush green. One could hear the cackle of rivulets and the melody of waterfalls. If there were clusters of trees at places there were also sandy expanses. All in all, it was a fascinating site.

There were animals with sharp claws. Seeing them Tommy's heart trembled. But they didn't care for him. They fought among themselves, their blood flowing. Tommy realized that he could not challenge these fearful beasts physically. He thought of a clever strategy. When one of the two fighting animals looked injured and vanquished, Tommy would pounce on it and run away with a piece of meat which he relished alone. Drunk in the happiness of victory they ignored him.

Tommy's good days had returned. It was Diwali every day. Neither jaggery nor wheat was scarce. Every day he had a new catch under the trees. He hadn't even imagined such heavenly happiness. He had reached heaven not by dying but by living.

In a short period, eating nutritious food injected new energy into him. His body became agile and well-rounded. Now he began to hunt smaller animals on his own. The animals were alerted to this and made efforts to turn him out from there. Tommy played a new trick. Sometimes he said to one enemy, 'That enemy of yours is planning to kill you.' To someone else he would say, 'That fellow calls you names.' The animals fell into his trap and fought among themselves. In course of time, it so happened that the big animals in the jungles disappeared. The smaller animals didn't have the courage to face him. Seeing his progress and his growing strength they felt as though this strange creature has been sent from the skies to rule over them. Tommy would reinforce this belief by showing his skill at hunting. He would declare proudly, 'God has sent me to rule over you. This is God's will. Stay comfortably in your own homes. I will not say anything. As a reward for my service I will only occasionally kill one among you. After all, I too have a belly. How can I survive without food?' He would now stride around the jungle casting proud glances around him.

The only worry that Tommy had was the emergence of a rival. He was always alert and armed. As the days went by and he grew more accustomed to a comfortable living, his worries increased all the more. Often he would get startled at night and begin chasing unknown enemies. He exhorted the animals, 'God forbid, you fall into the trap of some other rulers. He will simply smash you. I am your well-wisher; I always think about your well-being. Don't expect this of anyone else.' All the animals would reply in one voice, 'As long as we are alive, we will serve you.'

In the end, it so happened that Tommy did not have a single moment of peace. Throughout the days and nights he would pace along the bank of the river from one end to the other. He would run and run, pant for breath and then fall unconscious, but there was no relief from his worry, lest some enemy enter his territory.

But as mating season came, Tommy's mind became restless to meet his mate. He could not control his mind in any way. He remembered the days when he used to chase her with some of his friends in the lanes and alleys of the village. For two or three days he exercised patience but in the end his emotions became so strong that he was ready to challenge his destiny. Now he also prided in his energy and sharpness. He could easily vanquish two or three rivals.

But as he crossed over to the other side of the river his confidence began to wane like mist in the morning. His gait slowed down, his head came low and his tail shrunk, but at the sight of a lover he became emotional and began chasing her. The lover did not like his approach. She yelled her complaint. Hearing her voice several of her lovers converged there. They lost their temper at the sight of Tommy. Tommy was outnumbered. He had yet to decide upon his course of action when he was attacked from all sides with sharp teeth and claws. He didn't have the time to escape. His whole body was covered with blood. When he ran he had a whole bunch of the devils chasing him.

From that day, fear entered his heart. Every moment he feared that troops of attackers were coming to destroy his happiness and break his peace. He had had this fear earlier too, but now it was more intense.

One day he was terribly frightened. It seemed as though the enemies had arrived. He ran to the bank of the river and began to run from one end to the other.

The day ended, the night too, but he did not take rest. Another day came and went, but Tommy kept on making his rounds, without food or water.

Five days passed. Tommy's feet began to fester and his eyes darkened. Hunger made him weak and he fell down, but his worry did not leave him.

On the seventh day, Tommy, obsessed with his feeling of possessiveness, left for the other world. Not a single animal of the jungle came near him. No one uttered a word about him, no one shed a single tear upon his death. For several days vultures kept circling over his body. In the end, nothing was left except for his skeleton.

Translated from the Hindi by M. Asaduddin

The Price of Milk

1

Now you have midwives, nurses and lady doctors everywhere in the big cities. But in the villages, even today the delivery wards are looked after by sweeper women. And this situation is not likely to change in the near future. Babu Maheshnath, the zamindar of his village, was an educated man and well aware that the maternity hospitals needed modernization and improvement, but how could he overcome the obstacles that cropped up in the way? There was no nurse who would be willing to move to a village, and if somehow someone could be persuaded, she would demand such a hefty fee that Babu Sahib could do nothing but sheepishly return. As for a lady doctor, he could not even summon enough courage to approach her, for he would probably have been forced to sell off half his property to pay her fee. So when, after three daughters, a son was born, there was just Gudar and his wife to fall back on for assistance. Children generally are born at night. On a certain midnight, Babu Sahib's orderly made such a loud summons for Gudar that the whole neighbourhood woke up as well. It wasn't a girl this time and he was not going to call out meekly.

Gudar had keenly looked forward to and prepared for this day months in advance. What they feared was that there would be another girl. If that were so, they could get nothing more than the usual one rupee and a sari. He had quarrelled with his wife several times over this issue, and wagered on it. His wife would say, 'If it isn't a boy this time, I'll never show you my face, that's for sure. All the signs are that it'll be a son.' To which Gudar said, 'You wait and see, it'll be a girl. If it's a boy, I'll shave off my moustache.' Gudar was perhaps thinking that he would in this way strengthen his wife's exertions in favour of a boy and thus help bring this about.

Bhungi said to him, 'Now shave off your moustache, you bearded fellow. I told you a son would be born, but you never listened to me. You just stick to your own chatter. Today I am going to shave off your moustache and won't leave even a bristle.'

Gudar said, 'Well, you may do so, my dear woman. Do you think the moustache will never grow again? You will see that on the third day it will be just as it was before. But let me tell you, whatever you get, I am going to claim half of it.'

Bhungi made a dismissive gesture with her thumb and handing her three-month-old son to him, went out with the messenger.

Gudar called after her, 'Listen, where are you rushing off to? I too have to go to play the celebratory music. Who is going to look after this baby?'

Bhungi replied to him from where she was, 'Make him lie down on the ground and put him to sleep. I'll nurse him when I come back.'

2

Bhungi was thoroughly pampered at Maheshnath's house. In the morning, she got *harira*, for lunch she had puri and halwa, and was feasted again in the evening and then at night. And Gudar too had a hearty meal. Bhungi could nurse her own child just once or twice in the whole day and night, and so extra milk had to be arranged for him. Babu Sahib's son was the lucky one to drink Bhungi's milk. This went on till the twelfth day. The mistress of the household was quite healthy and strong but it so happened that there was no milk in her. The times when she had the three girls, her milk was so plentiful that it upset their stomachs; but for some reason this time she had no milk at all in her. So Bhungi acted both as a midwife and as a wet nurse.

The mistress would say, 'Bhungi, feed our son. Then you can just sit around and eat for the rest of your life. I'll have you given five bighas, rent-free. Even your grandchildren will live with ease and contentment.

While Bhungi's own child, unable to digest the extra milk, threw up frequently and was getting weaker day by day.

Bhungi would say, 'Bahuji, I'll have bracelets at the *mundan* ceremony, I insist.'

To which the bahu replied, 'Of course, you'll have the bracelets. Why the threatening tone? Will you have silver or golden ones?'

'Come on, bahuji! If I put on silver bracelets, who am I going to show them to, and who do you think they are going to laugh at?'

'All right, have the golden ones. I give you my word.'

'And at his wedding I'll have a necklace, and for my husband, silver wristbands.'

'All right, you shall have them. But God grant that we see that day.'

The household was presided over by Bhungi, after the mistress. The maids, cooks and the servants, all followed her command. So much so that even bahuji gave way to her. Once she even rebuked Maheshnath himself. He just laughed it off. There was some talk about Bhangis. Maheshnath had said: 'Whatever else may happen in this world, a Bhangi will remain a Bhangi. It is hard to civilize them.'

To which Bhungi had said, 'Master, it is the Bhangis who made others humane, how could it be the other way round?'

If Bhungi had shown such impertinence on any other occasion, would the very hair on her head have been spared? But today, Babu Sahib just chuckled and said, 'Bhungi's remarks are indeed full of wisdom.'

3

Bhungi's rule could not last beyond a year. Those who were sanctimonious objected to the boy being nursed with a Bhangi's milk, and Moteram shastri even suggested penance. The nursing was stopped, but the talk of atonement was just laughed off. Maheshnath admonished the shastri and said, 'So you say, shastriji. You talk about atonement. Until yesterday he lived off and grew up on the blood of the Bhangi, and now she has become polluting. What a wonderful dharma you have!'

Shastriji whipped his top-knot and said, 'It's true he was nourished on the Bhangi's blood. He's been brought up on her flesh. But that was in the past. It's different today. In Jagannathpuri the touchables as well as the untouchables all sit to dine in the same row. But it cannot be done here. During sickness, we eat food wearing our clothes, why, Babuji, we even eat khichri, but when we get better, we do observe the rules and customs. Don't we? Our dharma is unique.

'Does that mean the dharma keeps on changing, sometimes this way, sometimes some other way?'

'Yes, why not? The dharma is different for a king, the subjects, the rich and the poor. The royalty may eat what they like, and with whom they like; they can marry anybody they want; there are no restrictions for them. They are powerful people. It is the common folk who have to observe restrictions.'

So there was no atonement, but Bhungi had to step down from her pedestal. Of course, she got so many gifts that she couldn't carry them on her own, and she got gold bangles too. And, instead of one she got two beautiful saris—not merely as a formal gesture as when the daughters were born.

4

There was an epidemic of plague that very year and Gudar was the first one to fall victim to it. Bhungi was left alone, but somehow her household carried on. The people thought Bhungi will choose a partner. They noted how she talked with a Bhangi and received a certain Choudhury, but Bhungi just didn't follow anyone, nor did she go anywhere. Five years passed on and her son Mangal, despite his poor physique and being nearly always sick, started to run around. In front of Suresh, he looked a mere pygmy.

On a certain day, Bhungi was cleaning the drain at Maheshnath's house. A lot of sludge had accumulated over several months. The water had begun to form pools in the courtyard. She thrust a long, thick bamboo pole into the drain and shook it vigorously. All of her right hand was inside the drain. Suddenly she let out a shriek and as she withdrew her hand, out came a black snake slithering away. People ran after it and killed it, but Bhungi couldn't be saved. They had been under the impression that it was a harmless water snake and hence wouldn't be poisonous, and so they didn't care much. When the poison spread through her body and seized her, they found out that it was not a water snake but a venomous corn snake.

Mangal was now an orphan. He kept hanging around the doors of Maheshnath's house all day. There was so much leftover food that five to ten children like him could be fed on it. There was no scarcity of food. But he did feel bad when the food was dropped from above into his earthen bowls. Everyone else was served on fine plates, but for him there were earthen bowls!

Mangal might not have been aware of this discrimination at all, but he could see that the village boys made fun of him and insulted him. No one even asked him to join in their games. So much so that even the canvas rag on which he slept was untouchable for them. There was a neem tree in front of the house. Mangal made his home under it. All he had was a tattered canvas rag, two earthen bowls and a dhoti cast off by Suresh babu. But he found comfort at this spot. Mangal, who was lucky enough, lived through whatever season, scorching summer, freezing winter or torrential rains. He grew stronger than ever. And if there was someone he could call his own, it was a pariah dog of the village who, tired of being picked on by his fellow dogs, had taken refuge with him. Both of them shared the same food, slept on the same rag, they even had similar temperaments and understood each other pretty well. They never quarrelled.

The self-righteous people of the village were surprised at this tolerance shown by Babu Sahib. They thought that it was against genuine dharma that Mangal should have settled right in front of the house. It couldn't have been fifty cubits. *Indeed, if this sort of thing were to continue, one would think the end of all dharma to be at hand. We know a Bhangi too is created by God. We should do no injustice to him. Who doesn't know that? God is called by the name of Patitpawan, redeemer of the lowly. However, social propriety is something that has to be taken into account. Now we feel embarrassed even to approach that gate. We know, of course, that he is the master of the village but this is something one finds disgusting.*

Mangal and Tommy, the dog, were very close to each other. Mangal would say, 'Come on, Tommy, move over a little and sleep. Where is the space for me? You've cornered the entire rag.'

Tommy would whimper, wag his tail and instead of moving on, would get astride him and lick his face. Every evening he would go to his own house and cry. The first year the thatched roof fell in, the next year a wall collapsed and now only the broken walls were standing with their edges as spurs. That was all he had as his treasured property. His loving memories, his yearnings, would draw him to this ruin, with Tommy invariably accompanying him. Mangal would sit atop the edge of the wall, and recollect his past and dream of the future while Tommy would leap up again and again, unsuccessfully, trying to sit in his lap.

5

One day, several boys were playing together. Mangal came along but stood apart at a distance. Whether Suresh took pity on him or there were not enough players, it was hard to say. Whatever the case, it was suggested that Mangal should be included in the game. Who was going to see him here? 'How about it Mangal, will you play?'

Mangal replied, Oh no, bhaiya, if somehow the master were to see me, I'd be shooed off. What about you? You'll just walk away.'

Suresh said, 'Who's coming to look up here? Come on, we'll play horse and rider. You'll be the horse and the rest of us will ride on you and make you run.'

Mangal expressed his doubts, 'Tell me this, will I always remain the horse, or will I later be a rider too?'

It was a tricky question. No one had considered it. Suresh thought about it for a moment and said, 'Who's going to allow you to sit on his back? Just think of that. Aren't you a Bhangi?'

Mangal also stood his ground and said, 'When did I say I was not a Bhangi? But you too have been fed on my mother's milk. As long as I'm not assured of being a rider, I'll not be a horse. You people are very smart. You'll enjoy being riders and I will just be a horse all the time.'

Suresh scolded him and said, 'You've got to be the horse' and ran after him to catch him. Mangal quickened his pace.

Suresh, being overfed, had grown flabby and was soon out of breath.

Finally, he stopped and said, 'Come here, Mangal, be the horse, or else whenever I catch you, I'll give you a good beating.'

'You too will have to be a horse.'

'All right, I too will be one.'

'You'll just slip away. First you be the horse and let me ride. Then I'll be one.'

Suresh, indeed, wanted to play the trick. Then he told his companions, 'You see his treachery? He's a Bhangi, after all.'

All three of them closed in on Mangal and forced him to be a horse. Suresh promptly set himself on his back and clicking his tongue commanded him: 'Trot on, my horse.'

Mangal walked some distance but his back was breaking under the burden. Quietly, he drew his back and slipped out from between Suresh's thighs. As Suresh fell down with a thud, he started crying loudly.

Suresh's mother heard his cry. Whenever he cried she would pick up the sound as he had a peculiar cry, like the whistle of a narrow-gauge engine.

She told her maid, 'Look, Suresh is crying somewhere. Go and find out who beat him.'

Meanwhile, Suresh came in rubbing his eyes. Whenever he cried, he would invariably approach his mother and appeal to her. And his mother would offer him sweets or dry fruits, and wipe away his tears. He was eight years old, but a blockhead. Too much love had spoilt his wits just as too much food had ruined his body.

His mother asked him, 'Suresh, why are you crying? Who beat you?'

Suresh went on crying and said, 'Mangal touched me.'

His mother couldn't believe it. Mangal was so meek that he couldn't be expected to do any mischief. But when Suresh swore it was true she had to believe him. She called Mangal and scolded him, 'Why, Mangal, have you now started making mischief? Didn't I tell you never to touch Suresh? Don't you remember that? Come on, tell me.'

Mangal said in a low voice, 'I do remember that.'

'Then why did you touch him?'

'I didn't touch him.'

'Why was he crying if you didn't touch him?'

'He fell down and started crying.'

'A thieving and cheeky fellow!' the lady broke out, grinding her teeth. If she were to beat him, she would have to take a bath immediately. She would have had to take a stick in her hand, but the lightning current from the untouchable would penetrate her body through the stick. So, she heaped as much abuse on him as she could and ordered him to leave the house immediately, warning that if she saw him at their door she would suck his blood. 'You get all this free food, so that is why you think of mischief.'

It is doubtful that Mangal had a sense of shame, but fear did have a grip on him. He quietly picked up his pots, put his dhoti on his shoulder and walked off from there, crying. He wanted never to come back. At worst, he will die of hunger. So what? What is the point in living like this? Where else was there any shelter for him in the village? Who was going to give refuge to a Bhangi? He headed for the ruins where memories of better days might perhaps wipe away his tears, and he cried bitterly.

At that moment, Tommy came looking for him and the two of them forgot their miseries.

6

But as the daylight gradually faded, the shame in Mangal also abated. The hunger which unsettled his child's body grew stronger as it fed on his own blood. His eyes repeatedly turned towards the food bowls. There, by now, he would have been given Suresh's leftover sweets. *What is there to do here except to bite the dust?*

He took counsel from Tommy, 'Would you go and eat, Tommy? As for me, I'll go to bed hungry.'

Tommy whimpered as if to tell him, *This insult is to be borne throughout life. If you lose heart, what will happen? Look at me. If someone beats me with a stick, I let out a shriek, and then will follow the same person, wagging my tail. Bhai, both of us have been made the same way.*

Mangal said, 'All right, you go off. Eat whatever you get there. Don't bother about me.'

Tommy intoned in his dog language, *I won't go alone. I'll take you along.*

'No, I won't go.'

Then I won't go either.

'You will die of hunger.'

And do you think you'll stay alive?

'Who is there to weep over me?'

My situation is exactly the same. The bitch I had fallen in love with in autumn turned out to be unfaithful and she is now with Kallu. Thank God she took the pups with her or it would have got me into big trouble. Who was going to feed the five puppies?

The very next moment hunger devised a new stratagem.

'Why, Tommy, do you think our mistress will be searching for us?'

Of course, both Babuji and Suresh must have finished eating by now. The servant must have picked up the leftovers from their plates and will be calling out for us.

'There is a lot of ghee in the plates of Babuji and Suresh, and also that sweet thing, yes, the cream.'

All of that will be thrown into the garbage.

'Let's see if someone comes looking for us.'

Who will come? Are you a priest? They'll probably just call Mangal- Mangal once and no more. And the plate will be poured into the gutter.

'Well, then, let us go. But I will hide myself. If no one calls out my name I'll just come back. Take it from me.'

Both of them went back from the ruins and stood stealthily in the shadows at Maheshnath's door. But how could Tommy remain patient? He crept inside and saw that Maheshnath and Suresh were seated with their food plates. He quietly sat down on the porch, but was scared that someone would beat him with a stick.

The servants were chatting among themselves. One of them said, 'Mangal has not been seen today. The mistress scolded him. Maybe that is why he has run away.'

The other said, 'It's good that he's been kicked out. Otherwise, we'd have to face the Bhangi first thing in the morning.'

Mangal receded into more darkness. His optimism was running out.

Maheshnath finished his food and got up. A servant poured water over his hands to wash them. Now, he will smoke his hookah and fall asleep. Suresh, sitting by his mother's side, will sleep while listening to some story from her. Who is there to bother about poor Mangal? It is already late now, but nobody has called out for him, even by mistake.

For a while, he stood there disappointed. Then just as he heaved a long sigh and was about to go away, he saw a bearer carrying in a *pattal* with the leftovers of the meal.

Mangal came out of the darkness into the light. How could he now restrain himself?

The servant exclaimed, 'Arré, you were here? We thought you'd gone off somewhere. Come on eat it; I was going to throw it away.'

Mangal said in abject helplessness, 'I've been standing here for a long time.'

'Then why didn't you speak up?'

'I was afraid.'

'Well, eat this.'

He dropped the *pattal* into Mangal's outstretched hands. Mangal looked at him with eyes full of humble gratitude.

Tommy too had come out. Both of them started eating from the *pattal* under the *neem* tree.

Mangal patted Tommy's head with one hand and said, 'See, how there is this fire in the belly? What would we have done had these rotis not been thrown at us?'

Tommy wagged his tail.

'Suresh's mother has brought me up.'

Tommy wagged his tail again.

'They say that no one can ever fully repay the price of a mother's milk, whereas I am being paid for her milk in this way.'

Tommy wagged his tail yet again.

Translated from the Hindi by Satish C. Aikant

Defending One's Liberty

1

Mir Dilawar Ali had a pedigree bay horse. Though he would often claim to have spent half his life's earnings on it, it was really just an easy bargain from a regiment. Better still, you could say that it had practically been forced out of there. Perhaps the officers of the regiment did not feel like keeping it any more, and for that reason had decided to auction it.

Mir Sahib was a court clerk. He lived outside the city and had to travel three miles just to reach the court. This had him worried about a means of conveyance. The horse was a timely convenience, and so he bought it. Mir Sahib had been riding it for the past three years. Though it had no faults whatsoever, the animal seemed to bear perhaps an excessive measure of self-respect. Engaging it against its will or securing its services for demeaning tasks was simply out of the question. Anyway, Mir Sahib was unable to contain his joy because he had got a pedigree horse for a nominal amount. He brought it with him and tied it at his door. Now, finding a horse keeper was tricky. So, the poor fellow would himself stroke it gently for a while in the mornings and evenings. The horse probably felt pleased by such a gesture.

It was because of this that it never seemed discontented despite the exceptionally meagre amounts of food it would get. It had developed a sense of sympathy for Mir Sahib. This devotion to its master had made the horse quite weak. But it would happily carry him to the court at the appointed hour. Its leisurely gait indicated spiritual contentment, since galloping had always been against its natural sense of solemnity. There was a certain kind of wilfulness in its eyes. In its devotion to the master, it had sacrificed so many of its long-standing rights. The only privilege it was fond of now was its guaranteed Sunday rest.

Mir Sahib did not go to the court on Sundays. Rather, he would rub down his horse, give it a bath, and allow it to swim on Sundays. And this really delighted the horse. Otherwise, outside the court, it was tied to a tree and had to make do with dry grass. The hot winds scorched its entire body. But on Sundays, it would feast on fresh grass in the cool shelter of its shed. It thus considered resting on Sundays a prerogative, and it was quite impossible to deprive the horse of it. Sometimes, Mir Sahib would try mounting the horse to go to the market on Sundays, only to be utterly unsuccessful in such an enterprise. The horse would even refuse to wear its harness. Eventually, Mir Sahib made peace with his pet's obstinacy. He did not want to risk his limbs by hurting the horse's sense of self-respect.

2

Mir Sahib had a neighbour called Munshi Saudagar Lal. He, too, was somehow related to the court, though he did not hold a position there. No one had ever seen him reading or writing anything, but he was still highly respected in the company of lawyers and solicitors. He and Mir Sahib were close friends.

It was the month of June and the mania for weddings was at an all-time high. The obsessed ones went around the fireworks shops like Catherine wheels. The jesters and storytellers had their own way with people. The ones who carried palanquins acted like the stone gods—even presents and offerings did not melt their hearts. It was during this auspicious period, amidst this uproar, that Munshiji too decided to arrange for his son's wedding. After all, he was an influential person. He gradually made arrangements for everything that was needed, except for a palanquin. The Kahars had returned his advance deposits at the eleventh hour. Munshiji was furious. He even threatened them, but to no avail. So he helplessly decided that his son would ride a horse for the ceremony involving the groom's journey to the bride. The marriage party was scheduled to proceed at six. Around four o'clock, Munshiji went to Mir Sahib's place and said, 'Dear friend, why don't you lend me your horse so that it can carry the groom to the station? I can't seem to find a palanquin anywhere.'

Mir Sahib said, 'But don't you realize that it's Sunday today?'

Munshiji responded, 'Well, why won't I? But it's only a horse after all. Some way or the other, it can obviously manage a trip to the station. And it's not as if it's far off from here.'

'Be my guest, for what's mine is also yours. But I doubt if the horse will even be approachable today.'

'Oh, come on! A sound beating can even drive away demons. You're just afraid of it, and for that reason it behaves wickedly towards you. Once I mount it, it won't be able to shake me off no matter how hard it tries.'

'All right, suit yourself. And I'll owe you one if you can bend it to your will.'

3

The horse grew suspicious the moment Munshiji entered the stable. It neighed once as if to say he had no business spoiling its peaceful Sunday. The distant cacophony of the wedding's musical instruments made it even more anxious. When Munshiji tried to untie the horse, it got vigilant and began devouring the fresh grass with characteristic pride.

But Munshiji was also a shrewd one. He immediately ordered some corn from his house and put it before the horse. It had been days since the animal had had such food. It began eating with joy and looked gratefully at Munshiji as if implying its consent.

At Munshiji's house, the band was playing in full flow. The groom was elegantly dressed, waiting for the horse. The women of the suburb stood there, with the plates for the aarti ritual in their hands, waiting to see him off on his way to the bride's house. It was five in the evening. Suddenly, they saw Munshiji coming their way, along with the horse. The band members marched forward while someone got the rider's equipment from Mir Sahib's place.

It was decided that the horse should be strapped into its harness. But the very sight of its bridle made it turn away. Munshiji coaxed and urged the horse. He even patted its back and served it corn again. But the horse did not seem remotely interested and it was then that Munshiji lost his cool. He immediately whipped it several times. But when it still refused to be bridled, he unleashed the whip baton relentlessly on its nostrils. The beast started bleeding. It looked around helplessly with abject eyes. The problem was indeed a tricky one. It had never received such a thrashing before, and had always been Mir Sahib's favourite. He had never been so merciless towards it. Realizing that things would get even worse if it were to resist any further, the horse simply gave up. And that was all that Munshiji had hoped for. He quickly saddled the horse while the groom hopped on to it.

4

The horse woke up to its situation the moment the groom mounted it. It realized that to forfeit one's liberty for a small amount of corn would be like giving up one's birthright over mere trifles. *Why should I do unpaid work today when all this time I have been resting on Sundays? And there's no telling where these people will take me. The lad, too, seems like an expert rider. He'll spur me on, make me run, and whip me half-dead. And who knows if I'll even be given food or not?* Thinking thus, it decided not to take even a step further. *At worst, they'll beat me, but I'll throw myself down and roll over with the rider. They'll spare me then. And my master, too, must be somewhere around this place. He'll never want me beaten so much that I won't even be able to carry him to the court tomorrow.*

The women sang auspicious songs as soon as the groom mounted the horse. Flowers rained down on him. The marriage party began to march forward. But the horse was determined not to budge an inch. The groom spurred it on, whipped it, and even tightened the reins, but it seemed as if the beast's limbs had been firmly cemented into the ground.

Munshiji was so furious that he would have shot the beast had it been his own pet. One of his friends said, 'It's quite headstrong. This won't work. Try beating it from the back and it'll change its mind.'

Munshiji welcomed this proposition. He struck the beast several times from the back but to no avail. It only raised its forelegs towards the sky. Once or twice, it even attacked with its hind legs, which meant that it was not completely passive. Munshiji barely escaped the horse's retaliation.

Another friend said, 'Why don't you light a fire near its tail? The fear of the flame should do the trick.'

This proposition too was welcomed and the horse's tail was completely burnt. Twice or thrice, it jumped around the place in agony, but still refused to move forward. The horse was a true satyagrahi and the torment had perhaps further hardened its resolve.

Meanwhile, the sun had begun to set. Panditji said, 'Hurry, or the auspicious hour will soon pass.' But how could one hurry? It was not as if anything could be done about the matter. The marriage party had arrived outside the village. Women and children had assembled there in large numbers. People began murmuring, 'What kind of a horse is it if it doesn't take even a step forward?' An experienced person added, 'This beating won't do. Order some corn. Someone could lead the way with the corn in the nosebag. The bait should do the rest.' Munshiji even tried this idea, but he simply could not succeed. The horse did not want to trade its liberty at any price. Another man suggested, 'Give it some wine. It'll start prancing around once it gets drunk.' A bottle of wine was ordered. The liquor was poured into a trough and placed before the horse. But it did not even sniff at it.

What could one do now? The evening lamps had been lit and the auspicious hour had passed. The horse was quite pleased with itself, having successfully endured these various misfortunes. It actually revelled in the wretchedness and bewilderment of those who had disturbed its sense of peace. *I'll see what they do next.* It knew that it would not be beaten any more. People had already realized the futility of this. The beast was just contemplating its own skills and ingenuity.

Meanwhile, a fifth person said, 'Now, there's only one way out. Put a cart before the horse and place its forelegs inside it. That way it'll have to move its limbs the moment we begin pulling the wagon away. Once the forelegs start moving, the hind limbs will inevitably be set in motion. The horse will be walking before you know it.'

Munshiji's situation was that of a drowning man who clutches at straws. Two men fetched a cart while the groom tightened the reins further. A few people stood before the horse with sticks in their hands. Two more forcefully raised its forelimbs and kept them on the wagon. The horse had been under the impression that it could spoil even such a plan. But once the cart started moving, its hind legs were inevitably set in motion. It felt as if it was being carried away by an unstoppable water current. The more it struggled to anchor its limbs, the more it was at its wits' end. Everywhere, one could hear the chorus, 'It's walking! It's walking!' People clapped, guffawed, and made fun of the beast. This manner of contempt and ridicule was simply insufferable, but what could the animal do? Of course, it did not lose its patience. It reflected, *How far can they carry me away like this? I'll stop as soon as the cart comes to a standstill. I made a huge mistake putting my forelimbs on the wagon.*

The situation unfolded exactly as the beast had expected. Somehow or the other, people dragged the cart for a hundred steps or so and then gave up. Had the station been only another one hundred or two hundred steps further, they probably would not have lost heart. But it was still three miles away! Dragging the horse for so long was simply out of the question. The horse stopped as soon as the cart halted. The groom shook the reins again and tried to spur it on. He whipped it several times but the horse was equally up to the task. Its nostrils were bleeding, its entire body had been flayed and its hind limbs had suffered bruises. But the resolute beast stood its ground, defending its dignity.

5

The priest concluded, 'It's almost eight now and the auspicious hour is way past us.' The frail and wretched beast had won the day. Munshiji's anger, which had been driving him insane, now made him weep as well. The groom could not take a step further because it was considered taboo for him to keep his feet on the ground after the marriage procession had begun its journey. It would be a cause for criticism; one's reputation would be damaged, and the family name besmirched. But it now appeared as if walking was the Hobson's choice. Munshiji stood before the horse and said in a frustrated tone, 'Oh boy, thank your stars that you're Mir Sahib's property. Had I been your master, I would've given you a sound thrashing. That being said, today I've seen how even a beast can defend its liberty. I never knew that you'd stay true to your resolve. Son, you can get off the horse now. The marriage party must be nearing the station. Come, let's walk along. The dozen-odd men that we have here are all like brothers to one another. So, there's no cause for humiliation. And why don't you take off this fine coat of yours? People on the way will make fun of us if they realize that you're walking to the bride's house. And, you stubborn beast, come, let me take you back to your master.'

Translated from the Hindi by Shailendra Kumar Singh

Two Brothers

1

As the sun spread its golden rays in the morning, Yashoda fed rotis and milk to her two sons while they perched on her knees. Krishan was the older brother and Balram, the younger. The two boys took a mouthful each, skipped around for some time and then returned to their perch on their mother's knees. All this while they lisped the verses of a sensitive, old poet describing the plight of a child in the winter cold:

Deva, Deva, ghaam karo, tumhre balak ko lagta jaadh . . .
O God, O my God! Send me some warmth,
I feel so cold . . .

The mother called the two boys, kissed them and fed them big morsels. Just as there are pearls under the sea and bubbles on the surface, there was love in the mother's heart and pride in her eyes. The two brothers grew by leaps and bounds and played games together as they placed their arms on each other's shoulders affectionately. Krishan had a sharp mind,

Balram, a strong body. They loved each other deeply. They
went to school together and always shared their sweets.

Then, they got married. Radha, Krishan's consort, was
chatty, playful and had the eyes of a deer. Shyama, Balram's bride,
was healthy, tall, dark and sober. She was a soft-spoken woman.

Krishna was infatuated with Radha and Balram was
charmed by Shyama. But Yasodha couldn't strike a bond
with any of them. She was, in fact, unhappy with both. She
wished that Radha should acquire some traits of Shyama's
calm temperament while Shyama should learn something
from Radha's way with words. But much of her eloquence
and persuasive skill was wasted in the futile endeavour.

Both brothers had children born to them. The healthy
tree flourished and bore many a fruit; the frail one bore just
one fruit, that too pale and sickly. But both the brothers were
unhappy with their lot. Balram lusted after wealth while
Krishan longed for more children.

Lack of contentment in their own lots made the two
brothers envious of one another which soon turned into
jealousy. Shyama was always busy looking after the needs
of her children; she didn't have a moment to spare. Poor
Radha had to scorch herself before the kitchen fire or work
the grindstone. Her pent up anger and resentment would
sometimes burst forth in unpleasant words. Shyama listened,
felt offended, but kept quiet. But her silence only served to
inflame Radha's anger. Eventually, the cup brimmed over.
The deer, unable to find an escape route, turned upon the
hunter. Radha and Shyama fought fiercely and separated
like the two lines of a right angle. That day two kitchen fires
began to burn in the same house. Neither brother swallowed a
morsel of food that day. Yasodha spent the entire day crying.

2

Many years passed. The two brothers—who had once shared the same perch in the mother's lap, eaten from the same plate, suckled at the same breast—now could not bear each other's presence in the same house or even in the same village. To keep up appearances in public, they tried to conceal the burning embers of jealousy and ill-will by making pretences. But there was no brotherly affection between them anymore. They were brothers only in name. Normally, brothers are expected to be bound by deep affection. Their mother was still alive. She observed their gradual estrangement and felt deeply hurt. There was the same love in her heart but she no longer felt any pride in her sons. The flower was the same but it had lost its freshness.

When the two brothers were children, if one of them cried, the other, too, would begin to cry. They were simple and innocent then. Now, if one wept, the other laughed and enjoyed it. Now, they had become clever and wise. Earlier, when they had not developed self-interest, if someone teased them by threatening to take away one brother with him, the other rolled on the ground in protest and grabbed his shirt. Now, even if one brother was going to die, the other wouldn't care. They had learnt to act according to their self-interests.

Poor Balram's condition was really bad. His expenses were large and income low. Moreover, he had to keep up appearances. So, he had to bear his pain with a smile on his lips. His chest might be pierced with spots, but the clothes he wore had to be spotless. He had four sons and four daughters. It was difficult to meet the daily necessities which came at a high price. How far could the income from a few *payi*s of land go?

Getting the boys married was a matter of choice for him, but for how long could he put off his daughters' weddings? Two payis of land were sold during the first daughter's wedding. Even then, the groom's party walked away in a huff without partaking of the wedding feast. The second daughter was arranged to marry an old man. Shyama broke down in tears in the courtyard in full public view when she set her eyes on the groom. A year later, the third girl had to be married off. Of the tree that was once rich with foliage only the bare branch remained. But indigence has the same relationship with wealth as a hungry dog has with a piece of meat. Two years' *lagaan* was outstanding in his name. It was paid by pawning the daughter's jewellery, which provided a temporary reprieve. Radha had been waiting for this opportunity. She sent word to the girl's in-laws, 'You have no idea what's happening here. The girl's jewellery has vanished.' On the third day, a barber arrived at Balram's doorstep along with two Brahmins.

3

Once again, the poor man was in trouble. How could he raise the money? No land, no property, no orchard, no garden. He wouldn't be able to provide security to a moneylender. If any property remained, it was the two rooms in which he had lived all his life. And for which there were no buyers. Any delay in retrieving the jewellery would lead to disgrace. Helpless and bereft, he approached Krishan and said tearfully, 'Brother, I'm in dire straits, please help me.'

'Balu! To tell you the truth—I'm hard up for money these days,' Krishan replied.

But Radha intervened in her commanding voice, 'Oh no, you shouldn't make this excuse for them. Just because we eat our meals separately, we can't put at risk our family honour.'

Krishan looked at his wife with slight embarrassment. 'No, no, that's not what I meant. So what if we are hard up for cash, we'll have to find some way.'

'The jewellery was pledged for a little more than a hundred and twenty rupees, wasn't it?' Radha asked Balram.

'Yes, it comes to about one hundred and twenty-five rupees, including the interest,' Balram replied.

Krishan, who had earlier been reading the Bhagavadgita, became absorbed in it, once again. Radha took control of the business negotiations. 'It's a lot of money. If we had that much, there'd have been no problem. So we'll have to get it from someone else. And you know very well that the moneylenders never lend money without some kind of security.'

Balram reflected, 'If I had anything left to offer as security, why would I be knocking at your door? Are all the moneylenders dead?'

He said, 'What can I offer as security? All that I have now is this house.'

Krishan and Radha exchanged glances with faint smiles on their faces. They wondered if their dreams were coming to be true, and this wicked enemy was going to be rendered homeless. But this spiritual joy took on a sombre hue by the time it reached their lips. Radha said, 'No moneylender is likely to advance any money on the house. Had it been a city, the house would have fetched some rent. But in the countryside, no one will stay here even for free. Moreover, it's a joint property.'

Krishan was more circumspect in his use of words so that Balram wasn't scared away. 'I know a moneylender. Maybe, he can be persuaded.'

Radha nodded in approval of Krishan's timely intervention but said, 'Yes, it can be done only if you know the moneylender. However, getting more than sixty rupees will be difficult.'

Krishan felt desperate. Radha was being merciless while playing this game. He promptly added, 'Well, we can push him to hike it to eighty rupees, what else?'

Radha shot him a sharp look of reproof for his unseemly haste in clinching the deal. Then she said, 'If you can get us eighty, we should get the paperwork done right away. But moneylenders aren't blind.'

Balram had some inkling of the devious ways of his brother and his wife. He was surprised by the extent of their cunning and said, 'And from where will the rest of the money come?'

Radha flared up. 'You will have to find some other means to make up the shortfall. No one is going to give you a hundred and twenty-five rupees for these two rooms. If you are ready to settle for eighty, we can get the money from a lender, and you can get the paperwork done.'

But Balram refused to be conned so easily. He said with what appeared to be stupid obstinacy, 'What else should I worry about? If I had any jewellery left, I would have pawned it. I don't have anything left. If I have to face disgrace, it doesn't matter whether it is for ten or for fifty rupees. If I can save my honour by selling my house, it's fine. But I can't accept that my house should be sold and yet my honour is trampled to dust. My only worry is about the family honour. Otherwise, what can anyone do to me if I refuse? And truth be told, it's not my prestige that I'm worried about. Who knows me anyway? The world will laugh at you.'

Krishan turned pale; Radha, too, was flummoxed. But she knew the ways of the world and appreciated a bit of a banter. However, she had not expected such a move from a blunt fellow like Balram. She looked at him with appreciative eyes and said, 'Lala, sometimes you begin to talk like a child. Who on earth would give even a hundred and twenty-five rupees for this hovel? What to speak of a hundred and twenty-five, just get me a hundred and I'll sell my part of the house today. We have an equal share in the house, don't we? Yes, you will get eighty rupees for the house. The shortfall will have to be arranged by us. Your honour is bound with ours. It should not be lost. The money will be entered in a separate account.'

Balram was overjoyed. He felt triumphant. He said to himself, 'What I need is money. You can open not one, but ten new accounts, for all I care. As for the house, I'm not going to leave it as long as I live.'

He went back to his house happily. As soon as he was gone, Krishan and Radha started fiercely arguing about the different aspects of the deal and blaming each other for the bad bargain. At the end of a long harangue, they finally decided to focus on the positive side of the deal even if the profit was not substantial. The final consolation was—they would see how Shyama could ever behave like a queen in her house.

4

Why are noble sentiments so rare in the world? The creator of this world is the very embodiment of compassion, kindness and generosity. It is He who has endowed this world with heavenly gifts. God Almighty has created this world and subjected the large heavenly bodies and all the natural elements to the strictest rules. Yet, why has He allowed Man, a weak creature, such immense freedom? A freedom that he has always abused.

There were two bullocks standing outside Krishan's door. A strong bond of friendship existed between them, although the only relationship they had was being yoked to the same plough. And yet, a few days ago, when one of them was lent to Radha's family, the other one refused to put his mouth in the feeding trough for three entire days.

On the other side, here were two brothers, who had once shared the same lap and suckled at the same breast, who had become so hostile that they did not want to live under the same roof. Krishan would feel triumphant the day poor Balram would be rendered homeless and compelled to live in exile.

5

It was early morning. They mukhiya and the *lambardar* of the village appeared at Krishan's door. Munshi Datadayal, conscious of his status, sat proudly on a charpoy and was absorbed in preparing the mortgage deed. Again and again, he sharpened his quill but it did not improve his writing. Krishan's face was as radiant as the morning and Radha could barely contain her happiness. But poor Balram looked forlorn and lost in melancholic reflection.

The mukhiya said, 'It's truly a blessing to have a brother. If not, then it's as if one is surrounded by enemies. Krishan maharaj always looked after his younger brother.'

'Krishan maharaj saved all of Gokul, what to speak of his younger brother!' said the numberdar like a wise sage.

'Brother, that's what good sons should do,' the mukhiya added.

'Name of the mortgager?' called out Datadayal.

'Balram, son of Basudeo,' the elder brother replied.

'And the mortgagee?'

'Krishan, son of Basudeo.'

Balram looked at his elder brother, stunned. His eyes filled with tears. Krishan, too, looked at him but could not meet his eyes. This was the triumph of nature over human beings. The numberdar, mukhiya and mukhtar were perplexed. Was Krishan himself going to loan the money? But there was talk of arranging the loan from a moneylender. If there was money in the house, where was the need for a mortgage deed? Was there no trust between brothers! Arré, Ram! Ram!

Glances were exchanged. It took time for everyone present to get over their sense of shock. Shyama stood in the doorway. Though she had always been respectful towards Krishan, it was only respect for tradition that prevented her from giving her brother-in-law a piece of her mind that day.

When the old mother came to know all that had happened, tears streamed from her eyes flooding her shrivelled face. She looked up at the heavens and struck her forehead. She cursed her fate.

She recalled the scene from the past. It was a similar morning, bathed in golden sunlight, when her two adorable children sat on her knees and playfully ate their milk and rotis. Her eyes had glowed with pride then, her heart filled with hope and longings. But today—alas, there were tears of shame in her eyes and a huge burden of grief and regret in her heart.

She looked down at the ground and intoned softly, 'Oh Lord Narayana! Did I give birth to such sons from my womb?'

Translated from the Urdu by M. Asaduddin

The Bookbinder

1

In my office, there was a bookbinder named Rafaqat Hussain. His salary was ten rupees per month. He could also earn two or three rupees extra doing odd jobs. This was his total income and he was content with what he had. I don't know what his actual financial condition was, but he always wore neat and clean clothes and looked happy. Debt is normally an integral part of the life of people belonging to this category, but Rafaqat escaped its magic spell. There was no trace of artificial politeness in his way of talking. He was forthright in his views. If he saw any fault in his colleagues, he would point it out to them in a direct manner as he was very straightforward. Thanks to his straightforwardness, he earned much more respect than the people of this status normally get. He had a deep affection for animals. He owned a mare, a cow, a cat, a dog, many goats, and a few hens which he loved more than anything else. Every morning, he would get green leaves for the goats and grass for the horse. Although he had to visit the animal shelter almost every day, his love for his pets never diminished.

People used to make fun of his love for animals, but he never paid any heed to what they said. His love for the pets was selfless. Nobody saw him selling the eggs laid by his hens. He never sold any of his goats to the butchers. His mare was never bridled. The cow's milk was consumed by his dog. The goats' milk was meant for the cat. Rafaqat would drink only the leftover milk.

Luckily, his wife was a virtuous woman. Although her house was very small, no one ever heard her voice outside the house nor saw her standing at her doorstep. She never gave her husband sleepless nights by demanding jewellery or clothes. The bookbinder worshipped her. She would collect cow dung, feed grass to the mare, and make the cat eat sitting next to her. She loved the animals so much that she did not mind giving a bath to the dog.

2

One day, during the rainy season, when the rivers were in spate, Rafaqat's colleagues went fishing. Poor Rafaqat also accompanied them. The whole day, they enjoyed fishing. In the evening, when it started raining heavily, Rafaqat's colleagues decided to spend the night in a village, but Rafaqat left for his home. As it was very dark, he lost his way and kept wandering the whole night. When he finally reached his house in the morning, it was still dark but the door of the house was wide open. His dog came towards him moaning and lay down at his feet. A shiver ran down his spine on seeing the door wide open. Inside, it was unusually quiet. He called his wife twice or thrice, but there was no response.

There was a ghastly silence. He checked both the rooms and did not find her. Finally, he went to his stable trembling with an unknown fear as if he was entering a dark cave. In the stable, he saw his wife lying on her back. Her face was covered with flies. Her lips had turned blue and her eyes had turned into stone. The symptoms indicated that she had died of a snakebite.

The next day, when Rafaqat came to his office, it was difficult to recognize him. He looked as though he had been sick for many years. Completely lost, he sat in the office as if he was in a different world. In the evening, he got up and went straight to his wife's grave and sat there in the light of an earthen lamp till midnight as if waiting for his own death. God only knows when he returned home. From that day onwards, he would go to the graveyard every morning, sweep his wife's grave, place garlands of flowers on it, light some incense sticks and recite the Koran till nine o'clock. In the evening, he would repeat the same rituals. This had become his daily routine. He was now living in his own world. The outside world did not exist for him.

3

He remained in this state for several months. His colleagues sympathized with him. They did his work and avoided troubling him. People marvelled at his love for his wife. But a human being cannot live in his own world forever. The climate of that world does not suit him. Where in that world can one find such enchanting and pleasurable emotions? Resignation cannot bring ecstasy and joy filled with hope. The bookbinder would generally remain in his own world till midnight, but ultimately, he had to come out of that world and prepare dinner for himself and in the morning he had to take care of his pets. This work was an unbearable burden for him. Circumstances won over his emotions. Like a thirsty wayfarer in a desert, the bookbinder ran towards the mirage of conjugal pleasures. He wanted to see again that delightful show of life. The memory of his wife started fading against his strong desire of experiencing marital pleasures once again, so much so that there remained not the slightest sign of her memory after six months.

At the other end of his mohalla lived his office's peon, from whose family Rafaqat got a marriage proposal. He was extremely happy. The peon's status in the colony was no less than that of a lawyer. People made several attempts to guess his income. He himself used to say that when the government gave money to farmers to help them buy seeds, he had to keep a huge bag with him as his pockets were not big enough to hold his extra earnings. The bookbinder thought that fortune was finally smiling on him. He at once grabbed the offer the way children grab toys. All the marriage rituals were performed within a week and the new bride came home. A person who had lost all hope and was disenchanted with the whole world just a week back was sitting today on a horse with a wedding wreath on his head, looking like a new flower in bloom. It was a strange manifestation of human nature.

Before the week was over the new bride started showing her true colours. The Almighty had not blessed her with great beauty but to compensate the lack of it, He had given her a razor-sharp tongue to humiliate her husband and entertain her neighbours. For eight days, she minutely studied Rafaqat's behaviour and then told him, 'You are a strange creature. People keep animals for their comforts and not to make life miserable. Why do you let the dog drink the cow's milk and why let the cat drink the goats' milk? From today onwards, the milk must be brought home.'

The bookbinder couldn't say anything. The next day, he stopped giving gram to his mare. His wife would parch the gram and eat it with green chillies and salt. Every morning, she would drink fresh milk with her breakfast and make *tasmai* almost every day. As she belonged to a rich family, it was not possible for her to live without betel leaves. The consumption of ghee and spices increased in the house. In the first month itself, the bookbinder felt that his income was not enough to support his family. His condition was like a person who consumes quinine thinking it to be sugar.

The bookbinder was an extremely pious man. For two or three months, he endured that frightful pain. His face expressed his agony more than his words. He, who had been cheerful even in the most dire circumstances earlier, was now misery personified. Wearing dirty clothes, with dishevelled hair and an expression of deep sadness on his face, he lamented day and night. His cow had turned into a skeleton. His mare had become so weak that she was unable to move. Even the sneeze of a neighbour could scare his cat. The dog could be seen chewing on the bones picked from the garbage. Despite all that, this brave man did not leave his old friends. The biggest problem was his wife's sharp tongue due to which he sometimes lost his patience and his enthusiasm. He would often cry bitterly sitting in the corner of a dark room. Finding it difficult to be content with what he had, his broken heart took the path of extravagance. His self-esteem, which is a reward for being content with what one has, disappeared. He had to starve on many days. Now, he did not have a pot for storing water. In fact, he wanted to draw water from his well and drink it immediately so that it did not go waste. He was no longer satisfied with cold water and dry bread. He would get biscuits from the market and crave milk, cream and mangoes of good quality. How long can ten rupees last? He would spend all his salary in one week and then look for orders for bookbinding from private clients. Then, he would spend one or two days fasting, and after that he would start borrowing money. Slowly, the situation became so bad that from the first day of the month, he would start borrowing. Earlier, he used to advise others to spend sparingly. Now, others persuaded him to economize but he would say carelessly, 'Dear, let me eat what I am getting today, leave tomorrow to God. If I get something to eat tomorrow, I will eat, otherwise I will sleep hungry.' His condition was like a patient's who, after losing hope in medical treatments, stops exercising restraint on diet, and wants to eat as many goodies as he can before his death.

But he had not yet sold his mare and cow. One day, they were sent to the animal shelter. The goats also became victims of Rafaqat's extravagance. Due to his addiction to luxury foods, he owed money to the baker. When the latter felt that Rafaqat would not pay his outstanding dues, he took away all his goats while the bookbinder looked on helplessly. The cat, too, turned her back on him. In fact, after the departure of the cow and the goats, she didn't have any hope to get even a drop of milk, which was the last thread of love between her and her master. But, yes, the dog was still loyal to him owing to the good treatment he had received from him in the past. He had lost all his energy. He was no longer the same dog that never let any unknown person or a dog enter his master's house. He still barked but without moving and with his head tucked under his chest. It was as though he was cursing his fate.

4

One evening, I was reading a letter sitting near the entrance of my house. I suddenly saw the bookbinder coming towards me. A farmer would not be as scared to see a peon bringing a summons and a child would not be as scared to see a doctor as I was scared to see Rafaqat. I got up quickly and wanted to go inside the house and close the door, but the bookbinder was already there in front of me. It was not possible to escape. I sat on the chair, frowning, knowing very well why he had come. In fact, it is very easy to guess from his facial expression the intention of a person wanting to borrow money from you. He shows an unusual politeness and shyness which, once seen, can never be forgotten.

Without beating around the bush, the bookbinder told me the purpose of his visit.

I said rudely, 'I don't have money.'

The bookbinder bid me goodbye and left immediately. He looked so distressed and helpless that I felt sorry for him. The way he left without saying anything was so meaningful. It exhibited a deep sense of shame and remorse. He did not say a word but his face said a lot of things: 'I knew you would give this reply. I did not have any doubt about it. Despite that, I came here. I don't know why. Perhaps your kindness, your affection brought me here. Now I am going. I have no moral right to share my pain with you.'

I called the bookbinder, 'Come here. What's wrong? Why do you want to borrow money?'

The bookbinder saw a ray of hope. He said, 'What can I say? We have starved for the last two days.'

I advised him very politely, 'How long can you run your house by borrowing money like this? You are a sensible person. You know that everybody is worried about themselves. Nobody has extra money to spare. And even if somebody has, why should he get into trouble by lending money to someone. Why don't you try to improve your condition?'

The bookbinder said nonchalantly, 'It's all due to destiny. What else can I say? Things which I buy for the whole month last only a day. I am helpless before my wife's gluttony. If she doesn't get milk for one day, she will make a scene. If I don't bring her sweets from the market, she will make my life miserable. If I don't get meat for her, she will eat my flesh. I come from a respectable family. I can't afford to have a fight with my wife over matters related to food. I immediately get her whatever she wants. I pray to God for my death. I don't see any other way out. I have tried everything but without any success.'

I took out five rupees from my box and, handing it over to him, said, 'This is a reward for your self-respect. I did not know that you were so large-hearted and courageous.'

A person who endures family conflicts is in no way less brave than a soldier who fights on battlefields.

Translated from the Hindi by Faizullah Khan

Notes

The Story of Two Bullocks

First published in Hindi as 'Do Bailon ki Katha' in *Hans* (October 1931), and later included in *Mansarovar* 2 (1936). In Urdu, it was published in the collection *Aakhiri Tohfa* (1934) as 'Do Bail'. Now available in *Kulliyaat-e Premchand* 13 (2003).

Money for Deliverance

First published in Hindi as 'Muktidhan' in Madhuri (May, 1924), and later included in Mansarovar 2 (1936). Not available in Urdu. Transliterated from Hindi to Urdu for Kulliyaat-e Premchand 11 (2001).

The Sacrifice

First published in Hindi with the title 'Balidan' in *Saraswati* (May 1918), and later collected in *Mansarovar* 8 (1950).

It was published in Urdu with the title 'Qurbani' in *Prem Batteesi* 1 (1920). Now available in *Kulliyaat-e Premchand* 10 (2001).

The Roaming Monkey

First published in Hindi as 'Sailani Bandar' in *Madhuri* (January 1924), and later included in *Gupt Dhan* 2 (1962). Not available in the Urdu version. Transliterated from Hindi to Urdu for *Kulliyaat-e Premchand* 11 (2001).

Reincarnation

First published in Hindi as 'Purva Samskara' in *Madhuri* (December 1922), and later included in *Mansarovar* 8 (1950). Not available in the Urdu version. Transliterated from Hindi to Urdu for *Kulliyaat-e Premchand* 11 (2001).

Turf War

First published in Hindi with the title 'Adhikar Chinta' in *Madhuri* (August 1922), and later collected in *Prem Prasoon* (1924) and *Mansarovar* 6 (1946). It was published in Urdu with the title 'Fikr-e Duniya' in *Khaak-e Pawana* (1928). Now available in *Kulliyaat-e Premchand* 11 (2001).

The Price of Milk

First published in Hindi as 'Doodh ka Daam' in *Hans* (July 1934), and included in *Mansarovar* 2 (1936). In Urdu, it was published in the collection *Doodh ki Qeemat* (1937) with the eponymous title. Now available in Urdu in *Kulliyaat-e Premchand* 14 (2003).

The Hindi story is more incisive and critical than the Urdu story of the high-caste people and their dastardly treatment of the untouchables. The following passage which is a devastating indictment of the upper-caste prejudices against the lower castes is left out in the Urdu story:

> The self-righteous people of the village were surprised at this tolerance shown by Babu Sahib. They thought that it was against the dharma that Mangal should have settled right in front of the house. It couldn't have been fifty cubits. Indeed, if this sort of thing were to continue, one would think the end of all dharma to be at hand. We know that a Bhangi too is created by God. We should do no injustice to him. Who doesn't know that? God is called by the name of *Patitpawan*, redeemer of the lowly. However, social propriety is something that has to be taken into account. Now we feel embarrassed even to approach that gate. We know, of course, that he is the master of the village but this is something one finds disgusting.

Defending One's Liberty

First published in Hindi as 'Swatva Raksha' in *Madhuri* (July 1922), and later collected in *Prem Pacheesi* (1923) and in *Mansarovar* 8 (1950). In Urdu, it was published in *Naubahar* (1924). Now available in *Kulliyaat-e Premchand* 11 (2001).

Two Brothers

First published in Urdu as 'Do Bhai' in *Zamana* (January 1916) and collected in Urdu *Prem Batteesi* 1 (1920). Now available in *Kulliyaat-e Premchand* 10 (2001). It was published in Hindi with the same title in *Lakshmi* (September 1918), and later collected in *Mansarovar* 7 (1947).

The Bookbinder

First published in Urdu with the title 'Daftari' in *Kahkashan* (October 1919), and later collected in *Prem Batteesi* 1 (1920). Now available in *Kulliyaat-e Premchand* 10 (2001). It was published in Hindi with the same title in *Aaj* (1921), and later collected in *Mansarovar* 8 (1950).

The Urdu version is more expansive, fluent and rich in detail. The Hindi version is comparatively stark, and less fluent, shorn of interesting details that make the story in Urdu much more enjoyable. The aphoristic statement—'A person who endures family conflicts is in no way less brave than a soldier who fights in battlefields'—with which the Hindi story ends is missing in the Urdu story.

In the Urdu story, the reader gets to know that the bookbinder's colleagues in his office contributed a sum of money to meet the domestic expenses of Rafaqat, the protagonist, for a month. The Hindi version is silent about this. It seems that the Hindi story is an abridged version of the Urdu story. As the details are woven into each paragraph, they cannot be extracted in a coherent way. The full extracts that have been left out in the Hindi version are as follows:

Although Rafaqat had retained his outspokenness, no one now appreciated it. It was now treated as a waffle, like the harangue of a helpless widow. An insecure person is quick to take offence. One day, when some of his neighbours made some funny remarks about his new wife, he lost his temper. He was bare in his upper body and was wearing tattered pyjamas. He was in a rage, the veins in his throat dilated and his ankles aflutter. His addressees were sitting and playing cards, scarcely paying him any attention. It was as though a dog was barking. He had reached the lowest state of degradation where people treated even his anger with contempt.

. . . Once, at my initiative, the office colleagues, out of sympathy, contributed money and bought him provisions for a month. But the provisions meant to last a month disappeared in a week. The rice was bartered for mango, dal for jamun. The oven was lit three times a day, and then . . . the same story of starvation and want. Eventually, people lost all sympathy for him, so no one lent him even a paisa now. He stood there praying and blessing people, but no one even cared to look at him.

. . . 'Spend less than you earn, however compelling the circumstances. And why do you start borrowing from the first day of the month? Thinking of you, once I had arranged for a month's provisions for you. But you have gone back to your old ways. You were a reasonable person. You know very well that people do not always have ready money in their hands. Everyone has his own needs to take care of. And even if someone has money, why should he lend and thus invite trouble for himself? You have to go begging to ten persons to get one favourable response.

How embarrassing is all this! What is the matter with you, after all? You have been reduced to this condition for the last two-and-a-half years. Earlier, you looked so contented.'

Extract translated from the Urdu by M. Asaduddin

Note on Translators

Anuradha Ghosh teaches in the Department of English at Jamia Millia Islamia, New Delhi. Her specialization is in the area of literature, cinema and culture studies. Presently, she is working on an Indian Council of Social Science Research project on the Muslim question in Bengali and Malayalam cinema.

Faizullah Khan is associate professor of French at Jamia Millia Islamia, New Delhi.

Satish C. Aikant is former professor of English at HNB Garhwal University and a former fellow of the Indian Institute of Advanced Study, Shimla. He has been a visiting professor at Ecole des Hautes Etudes en Sciences Sociales, Paris, and the editor of *Summerhill: IIAS Review.*

Shailendra Kumar Singh is pursuing his PhD from Jamia Millia Islamia, New Delhi. He has a master's in English literature from Hindu College, Delhi University. His research interests include peasant narratives, gender studies and Premchand's literary corpus.

Shradha Kabra is a PhD student of English at Jamia Millia Islamia, New Delhi. Her areas of interest are English studies and cultural studies.